Thomas Toke Lynch

Memorials of Theophilus Trinal

Thomas Toke Lynch

Memorials of Theophilus Trinal

ISBN/EAN: 9783337094317

Printed in Europe, USA, Canada, Australia, Japan

Cover: Foto ©Raphael Reischuk / pixelio.de

More available books at **www.hansebooks.com**

MEMORIALS

OF

THEOPHILUS TRINAL,

STUDENT.

By THOMAS T. LYNCH.

Fourth Edition.

"God hath not given us the spirit of Fear; but of Power, and of Love, and of a
Sound Mind."—PAUL.

LONDON:

JAMES CLARKE & Co., 13 & 14, FLEET STREET,

1882.

PREFACE

TO THE SECOND EDITION.

I COULD not write a Preface to the first edition of this Book. It was better to let such a Book of the Heart speak for itself. I could not have said about it what would satisfy myself or any one else; and I might have spoken with awkward and tremulous intensity, or with an appearance of pride. For I felt the faults of the Book; felt, too, its worth, and know that it was part of the fruit of much arduous Thinking, and other Endeavour, continued through many years. Valuable and endeared to me, how could I but wish it might be so to others? Yet to solicit favour or to ask abatement of censure I should have thought alike vain and dishonouring. But now that the Book has found favour and friends, and is going forth again, not sanguine, but with the hope of fresh life and extended friendship, I may say a word; if only to express my thankfulness that Trinal's Verse and Prose have been so well received, and my hope that these Memorials will, as a Hand-book for the Practically Meditative, so help minister composure and suggestion, that their many editorial and other defects may be, not forgotten, but forgiven for the sake of what they offer.

There is much in these pages that will win its way to the " understanding heart " at once, if at all : but there are, also, what to many will seem . " dark sayings ; " and of these I venture to hope that they are as Dark Lant-horns, and that Attention, as the touch of a spring, may open and win from them a friendly and useful light.—The Book too may seem, as one private critic and wise friend says, " all middle," and it has indeed neither the methodic

form of Treatise nor Story; it is rather a book
Aphoristic in manner and style; and asks for
itself the benefit of these words from Lord Bacon:
"Aphorisms, representing a knowledge broken,
do invite men to inquire farther; whereas methods, carrying the show of a total, do
secure men, as if they were at farthest."

Trinal is no mere disintegrator: in Theology
he is Reconstructive; in all thought aims to be
Reconciliative, a Harmonist.   And such are
the tendencies of these Memorials.   " The
negative work of the Iconoclast," he writes too,
" is not the only or the highest negative work.
The Statuary is negative with his chisel.   The
Iconoclast says, ' Thou shalt not be,' and
shatters what is worthless and delusive with
his hammer.   The Statuary says to each chip
of marble, ' Thou shalt not be here,' but he
removes it under the guidance of an existent
Positive Idea, and one that may perfect itself
in process of the work.   He acts Negatively
but Creatively too."

And now, with the hope that the Reader may find the Verse and Prose, as Trinal has it,

> " Twins, a sister and a brother,
> Each the dearer for the other,"

and commending to his attention these other words of Trinal's—" Prose is the Ship of my soul ; Verse, the Life-boat. I had been lost often, but for the Life-boat. Give me the Ship for company and cargo, but not without the boat for safety, my companions' and my own,"

The Editor

Bids him for the present

Farewell.

Camden Road, London.
May, 1853.

CONTENTS.

CHAPTER VII.

CHAPTER VIII.

INDEX

TO THE POEMS.

"WISDOM IS A LOVING SPIRIT."

Book of Wisdom.

DARK with unutter'd Thought and Love,
  Oft is the heart a clouded sky;
Come rains of speech, and then above
  Hope shows its bright infinity:
Then fall the showers on the earth,
  Then fall the showers on the sea;
Aiding in Use' and Beauty's birth,
  Lost in the dark immensity.

So, Heaven above thee is the lighter,
  O Book! if honour'd thou to yield
Such drops as shall make earth the brighter,
  By help to thirsting flower and field;
Such drops as like a shower may fall
Into Truth's oceanic All:
And thus wilt thou the bounties of the Main
By work and reverence, return again.

MEMORIALS

OF

THEOPHILUS TRINAL.

PRELUDE OF POEMS.

LIKE the stars that show their grouping
　　When the Dusk subdues the Day,
Are the Truths that shine together
　　ᵥhen Thought has quiet sway.

Like the sunshine on the waters,
　　Like the light within the dew,
To our Heart and to our Hoping
　　Is an old truth utter'd new.

Like the rich and heavy bunches,
　　Like the bright and strengthening wine,
Are the weighty words of Wisdom,
　　And the Poet's loving line.

B

And the Powers that play in Fancy
  Can a holy earnest show,
As the colours of the Bubble
  Shine serenely in the Bow.

———•———

Oh, sweetest flower of darkest spot,
  Bean-blossom, favourite of the fields,
The heart that solemn sorrow shades,
  Like thee the richest fragrance yields.

Bean-blossom, private to the bee,
  But public on the summer wind;
The heart whose hidden store is most,
  Has freest gift for all mankind.

Bean-blossom, dying, thou wilt leave
  A legacy of wholesome food;
So, tender, thoughtful hearts bequeath
  A wisdom plain, for daily good.

———•———

Thought and Sorrow are akin,
  Of Sorrow, Sanctity is born;
Sanctity outcasteth Sin,
Welcome Hope it bringeth in,
  Crown'd with blossoming thorn.

Musing, I grieved at close of day,
 Grieved, and my soul would purify;
I stood till golden clouds were grey,
Hills melted into mist away,
 Alone with stars was I.

" Draw near, and I will nearer draw,"
 Thus hath He spoke, I said, and wept:
I felt the glory that I saw,
I felt the ancient love and awe;
 The promise: it was kept.

With flowers upon a bleeding brow,
 Hope at morning came to me:
Sweet tender Hope, unknown till now:
O Hope! the thorn has bloom'd, and thou
 Comest, and strength with thee.

Thorn without flowers; flowers on the thorn;
 Then thornless everlasting bloom.
Three crowns: the first when Faith hath worn,
And Hope, the next, with brow still torn,
 Love shall the last assume.

While little boys, with merry noise,
 In the meadows shout and run;
And little girls—sweet woman-buds—
 Brightly open in the Sun;
I may not of the world despair.
 Our God despaireth not, I see,
For blithesomer in Eden's air
 These lads and maidens could not be.

Why were they born, if hope must die ?
　Wherefore this health, if truth shall fail ?
And why such joy, if misery
　Is conquering us, and must prevail ?
Arouse ! our spirit may not droop,
　These young ones fresh from heaven are :
Our God hath sent another troop,
　And means to carry on the war.

CHAPTER I.

MAN AND THE BIRD.

OH ! what would it avail to have
   The heart of bird, without his wing ?
It were a woe to view the height,
   Yet powerless be to rise and sing.

And what were it a wing to have,
   Without an eye far-seeing, bright ?
The spaciousness of ample heaven
   Were but a prison, without light.

And what, without the heart of bird,
   Were it to have both wing and eye ?
The love must be as is the life,
   To use its powers rejoicingly.

Truth for the bird his eye discerns ;
   By birdly hope his wing is strong ;
And full delight in birdly good,
   Makes utterance for itself in song.

Man hath a large unresting heart—
His good he is pursuing still ;
And reason is his wondrous eye—
His mighty wing, it is his will.

Like down by lightest breezes stirr'd
Would be his heart, if he were blind ;
But, reason-guided, he can soar,
And free-adventuring breast the wind.

And though the heart may prisoner seem,
When man is weak for flight and song ;
Yet soon aloft on rested wing
He sweeps exultingly along.

Self-active, wisely, and in love,
Man greater grows, already great ;
His heart will swell, his wing expand,
His eye will brighten and dilate.

But vain alike were wing and eye,
Could eye and wing be found alone ;
What is it but the heart of love
That differences man and stone ?

Of thinking, acting, loving, vain
Were any two without the third ;
But by the union of the three,
Man soareth heavenward, like the bird.

Sometimes, when creation, as a grand, most
clear and fair firmament, is loftily and protect-

ingly about our spirit, we rise into wide regions
of thought, as on wings of eagles, to disport
ourselves in the free sunshine of heaven, our soul
breathing light as our body breathes air; then,
as a dark and darkening cloud, the sin and misery
of man confront us, and, as if smitten by a light-
ning-stroke from thence, we fall to the ground,
groan for a while, and then lie long benumbed
into a torpor of silence.

Human nature, like ancient Job, sits foul and
sore with disease, spirit-worn and weary with
incessant strivings of heart. The Philosophies,
as friends, come with their sympathy and wisdom; but their words are dark clouds edged
brightly, which reveal the splendours of Truth
behind them, but disclose not the orb—and, to
the parched heart, they are but as clouds, with
a wind indeed, but without rain. But after the
discoursings of philosophy with human nature,
there is heard the voice of God saying, "I am;
behold My works; hope and believe."

As experience enlarges, spiritual questions
accumulate, till at the last they pass into one
great question concerning the world and human
life, which the heart expresses not in words, but
which fills it with a mute agony of wonder. To
this question there is no answer, nor hope of

any, till the voice of God is heard, saying, " I am." This voice, from a whisper, rises till it has the " sound of many waters."

Happy are we if we believe and feel that the " Man of sorrows," and of success after sorrows, Jesus, the Son of God, is still His real and sufficient representative. He is God's surety to the world. He, bearing the sins of the world, bears also its difficulties. In the faith of Christ have the men of many generations found fixed standing-places, immovably secure. In Him they have heard the voice—"I am." "Here we rest," they have said ; " our God, we will not distrust Thee." He bears the great golden key of love that shall unlock the secret of the world. This key is as key of escape from a prison, key of entrance to a palace. Oftentimes in life we may seem as those who struggle in a wide storm-sea, knowing their strength only by the greatness of their ineffectual efforts. Yet are we safe. For though we may feel as if rather drifting in a slight skiff over boisterous waters, than making way over them in a strong vessel —yet if, after many days, Columbus found the land which reason taught him to hope for, much more shall we reach the country promised to the faithful.

Thus wrote Theophilus Trinal as he sat at his desk at evening, after a day of studies. "Words of sighing," said he, "may be as the sighing of the evening wind—soft, but healthful. Yet too much of a musing too sorrowful should be avoided, even as the damps of evening are."

"For each day," said Theophilus, "we should seek salubrity and sanctity. Minutes and half-hours of prayer and Divine meditation will give sanctity; and, as for me, my aids to health and contentment are, music, mathematics, and cold water. These make the days salubrious. Music ventilates my spirit. My ears become the opened windows of my soul, and sweet airs enter—airs from the everlasting hills of hope, across which lies the heavenly country. Mathematics dispel my fogs and vapours, like a frosty wind. Meditative thought, that as a western wind brought me feelings so mildly glowing, and of such gentle flow, brings me, if it continues too long, haze, gloom, and slumberousness. The clear, cold mathematics relieve me. Then, how bright and grand the old stars of truth become! How strong and how warm I feel! And as for cold water, though I still step often into my tub with fear and trembling, I have my reward, for I step out girded for employments; my mind is as an instrument fresh tuned, and I come to my breakfast hungry and practical."

Our book is not a history. Glimpses we shall give of Theophilus in different scenes; but our chapters will consist of his thoughts and poems, and meditations and observations. Next, then, in this first chapter, there comes a poem upon Thoughts—and then the chapter closes with some meditations upon Meditation.

THOUGHTS.

How comes a Thought ?—
  Even as the dew,
Which falls not in a visible drop,
  But the still night through
Gathers upon the flower-cup,
  Life to renew.

How unfolds a Thought ?—
  As a bud of spring,
Which in itself contains a branch
  Leaf, and blossoming—
A bough on which a happy bird
  May rest and sing.

How abides a Thought ?—
  As a heavenly star,
Which seen by us, but not controll'd,
  Burns in its sphere ;
Veil'd often, but by passing clouds,
  Our own eye near.

Hath a Thought a voice ?—
  As sweet as bird,
Whose melody, in a dusky wood
  With wind unstirr'd,
Spreading, like brightness from a lamp,
  All around is heard.

Will a Thought leave us ?—
  Even as the moon,
Which from fullest beauty failing,
  For a while is gone—
To come again in softest light,
  Surely and soon.

Doth Thought propagate ?—
  Like polyp of the sea,
Fashion'd of buds into a form
  Of strangest beauty ;
Each bud in stillness opens—each
  May parent be.

What power has a Thought ?—
  The power of an eye,
Whose expression the soul changes,
  As the sun the sky ;
There are sudden lights, a slow dawn,
  Shadows that fly.

Can a Thought be lost ?—
    Lost but as rain,
Some of which falls on a lily
    Without a stain ;
While some anew, dispersed in air,
    Will fall again.

What is Thought to life ?—
    As air to a tree,
Which, through summer and through winter,
    Works invisibly ;
Building up the trunk and branches
    With solidity.

ON MEDITATION.

All men need truth as they need water. If wise men are as high grounds where the springs rise, ordinary men are the lower grounds which their waters nourish. But it is given to all men to have a place of fountains within themselves. From a man's heart may streams flow at which he may drink and refresh,—streams which will fertilize the ground of his daily labour, and will sustain and invigorate activities, whether of a robust or a tender growth. The currents, sometimes calm and transparent, at others swift and sparkling, at others, again, pure, but dark

from their depth, will delight him with their
varying flow. Happy are we when the flow
of our thoughts is not turbid and defiled. With
many it is usually or often thus, and with all it
is sometimes thus. Sometimes, too, our mind
is as hard, bare rock, and the world around us is
as sand. Then meditation may be a rod of
wonder; with it we make the rock yield waters,
and the desert blossom and rejoice. But meditation becomes charged with this power only by
frequent use; and, besides, works its work now
speedily, and now slowly. And often in times
of perplexity and sorrow we require continuous,
unrelaxing endeavour, before by inward effort
we can work an inward change. At such times
we can best secure partial returns of brightness
and warmth by the aid of the Scripture utterance and histories, or other utterances and
histories of those who have thought, felt, and
striven divinely, yet with human shadowings,
backslippings, and inequalities. If on these we
fix our mind, as in gazing men fix the eye, we
shall be as those who mount a hill in mist that
dims the sunlight and hides the beauty around,
but on whom breaks suddenly the vision of
valleys before them, covered with light—deep,
fruitful, and serene ; and, as they turn to look

upon the ascending path, behold that also is changed, and all is alike lovely.

Every thoughtful man has, as in some large, awful, twilight chamber, communion with spirits, which converse with him in a peculiar language that he cannot teach to other men, yet which introduces changes into the idiom of his discourse. Let him beware that he neither be, nor needlessly appear, as spiritually a barbarian. Deep spiritual wisdom, when its utterance is principally for the mind, must be uttered clearly; when principally for the heart, with tenderness, or with a shadowed majesty. All wise words are of the heart's integrity; but not all either can or should be at once clear to the hearer. But they who have seen a vision, though they can but hint darkly and vaguely at its wonder and manner of appearing, yet, if it was a heavenly vision, will show this by their practicalness; they will be "obedient,"—speaking directive words according to the mind of the vision, or kindling, by urgency and earnestness, lamps of aspiration, according to its heart.

Man has within him both garden and farm : he may have delight and refreshment in meditation, and he may know the laborious toil of thought. He who seeks truth, must give much painful heed to things that grieve and perplex the soul. He must *feel*, if he seeks worthily to know, and is to find a knowledge worth the knowing. Often in the beginning of meditation, truth is with us, and above us, as the bright-coloured firmament of evening with its blending hues; but deep seriousness soon shadows the spirit, the colouring gradually vanishes, and when the immovable, majestic stars appear, it is in a dark heaven that their fires burn. These are fires that burn for us while we are musing— fires of primal and enduring, but still far-off-seen truths. But in pure thought also, we, as partakers of the Divine nature, become ourselves "fathers of lights,"—lights for the temple, the home, the highway, or the stormy seas.

The thoughtful man, labouring inwardly as on his estate, that he may possess himself of sentiments and judgments, as capital and resources of his own in his action and intercourse, constitutes his heart as a smelting-furnace for truth-ore. He who has thought for himself depends not exclusively on others; and yet neither will he depend exclusively upon himself. He deals with raw materials of thought, and knows processes of preparation; but he does not manufacture for all his needs. He buys at the market of wisdom; but when he buys, he judges well and carefully of worth, and can detect adulteration. He can look around the world, and discern uses in things that other men will despise. He can scheme, invent, and combine for himself. Having thoughts of his own, he will speak of truth and opinion generally, as one who has seen and examined—not merely has heard the report of other men. The reflective man will see in his very pathway, illustrations, oppotunities, and phenomena, for which it might once have seemed necessary to go far and to search widely. It is a fault in life as great as obvious, that we see not, or heed not, how principles that we honour and profess to obey may be, and are, applied or violated in our common conduct. He who meditates will be able to see this, and to show it. Accustoming himself to think, he will soon find shining within him, as central suns, certain great fixed principles. In their light will he see the things of his life, and of the world. His whole being will almost unconsciously become orderly and vivified, changed, and glorious, under the influence of these suns.

The thinking man, too, as another good result of his thoughtfulness, will get to feel how truly and impressively best thoughts and inward visions are gifts of God. When our "views," as we significantly say, are largest, most solemn, or most beautiful, we are often conscious rather of being in a state than of making an effort. By effort, perhaps long and painful effort, we came into this state. But after aspiration and endeavour, now comes inspiration. We have made this a word for ourselves—Lift the eye, and let the foot follow. We saw the heights, or knew that there were heights, if on them a cloud rested ; we climbed, and now there is presentment of the wide and varied vision. A spiritual thinker will recognize God in his own true and pure thoughts. And when he finds rising within him beautiful growths, increasing freely, he will say, "The earth tilleth not herself, yet bringeth she forth fruit and flower of herself." He will regard thoughts as having vitality of their own, derived from the great, original, creative Life.

Our thoughts and states vary with our life and action. If wise, we live and move in God, that He may live and move in us—as God, the guide and friend. And whether wise or no, that

c

which groweth up within us, and moves in us brightly or darkly, is in a true sense God's working and award. But though thoughts in the mind, as flowers in the field, grow up, man knoweth not how, yet has man a true agency in the product of thought. Eyes and the world of vision are of God; but it is for man, in true though varying measure, to choose whether he will see, and what he will see—to observe those laws according to which grace or distortion will meet his view. Man may choose between the true and the beautiful on the one hand, the false and the hideous on the other; but God determines the terror or glory of the visions, their greatness and variety. We need to feel combinedly, according to a law growing gradually clearer, our dependence upon God and our distinct personality and answerableness. We have real, separate powers; of which we must make real, strenuous use. The kind of results obtained depends chiefly upon ourselves; the greatness of these, on God. Human thought and action lead to great things, because of the greatness of the world and its Creator. By our will, we do acts that are as fore-provided signals for the operations of Divine strength. From the meditations of universal man, which are, in such large part, of God's working and bestowment, have risen and fashioned themselves the structures, institutions, and habitudes of external life ; so that the great things and the wonderful of the world, are as a Divine creation. In part, because of man's free evil work and its effects, the world lieth in wickedness, as God would not have it lie ; in part, because of God's working in and by man, the world marches on in the ordered course of its journey, and the eras are as God would have them be. The thinking find the world not according to their mind wholly, as it is not according to God's mind wholly. But the thinking may recoil from that patient work, to which it is according to the mind of God they should gird themselves. Facts and necessities are around us, which, for work's sake, and for conscientious judgment's sake, require our direct and careful regard. These must we consider with fixity and heartiness, if we would see best inward visions, and enjoy the glory, the wonder, and the luxury of imaginative, spiritual thought. The daily practical and the meditative are as two gardens; both are beautiful, but one is magical. In the first are common plants, which we must diligently tend and cultivate. In the second, among flowers also for cultivation, flowers of new and most changeful beauty are ever rising spontaneously. In this second garden may we walk, having duly cared for the first. It is a garden of surprise and delight ; for we have but to think of some common flower, when straightway it arises before us, as transfigured, in exquisite beauty; and all around it as a centre, new vegetative forms spring up, different but analogous. These two gardens have to each other curious and important relations. The perfection of either can alone be secured by a due regard to both. If we regard only the magical one, the magic becomes less wonderful, and will soon cease to surprise and delight us. And if we regard exclusively the common one, it becomes alarmingly magical ; familiar plants assume a noisome aspect, and around them rise others uncouth and terrifying. Our care must be—for our common ground, that its productions be abundant and healthy; for our magical one, that its growths be numerous and beautiful. This is best secured by periods of toil in the first, alternating with shorter periods of recreation and delight in the second. Accurate thought on definite subjects can alone give freedom and variety to general meditations ; conscientious practicalness alone insure us best visions and revelations.

CHAPTER II.

Upon a windy evening Theophilus Trinal paced his study in earnest meditation. "Now and then a sigh he stole," though it was evident his hours of study had not wanted the refreshment of music. On the desk of his opened piano stood Handel's fine song, "Bacchus, ever fair and young." Theophilus would say, he was too catholic to regard every thing Bacchic as profane. A friend of water, he had yet a good word for the old transgressor—wine. "Wine is a publican," he said, "not without heartiness and truth, though a passionate doer of many mischiefs. Man's use and abuse of wine has deep meaning. Man would have his heart burn with a furnace heat and brightness—he would feel his very highest and best. Dulled and fettered with trouble and toils, he seeks glow and freedom. But he would get his good and forget his pain, when patience and wisdom say admonishingly, Not now—not yet. Some wine of inspiring gladness he longs for. To be glad and strong, surely this is his fitting estate. But he entereth not in by the right way. He climbeth up another way, and is cast out as a robber—hurt and disgraced. He bloweth his fires first bright, then dead. His wines, that make him for an hour less a sorrower, make him for days more a sinner. He would be as a god in joy and fulness of heart, before he is as a god in labours and holiness. Of man's need, his sin, his destiny, his greatness, his folly, and his joys—of all these, wines of the grape and wines of pleasure speak many and strange things. Bacchus, the poetry god of inspiring gladness, has somewhat to say for himself in answer to what the world has to say against him." The book Ecclesiastes lay open on Theophilus' table. Perusal of this had formed part of his occupation. "This book of the Preacher has value," thought he, " rather for its frank and large statement of difficulties, than for the light it sends upon or through them. It is a book of questionings—the questionings of your own heart 'writ large.' And it is good to find such sympathy as this for your questioning moods. He who feels the question is the man most likely to gain or approximate to the answer, or best prepared to receive it. But let us often affirm the clearness that is in God, whilst yet in the dusk ourselves. We shall find that as the All is at last to be lit up with an interior light, so again and again particular difficulties are revealed and transfigured by the partial illuminations of interior meaning."

The mind of Theophilus, at the time we introduce him pacing his room, was somewhat stormy and disturbed, like the evening. He was meditating Christianity, its present lesson and worth, and its everlastingness. He said within himself, "Christianity, if a tree, is a trained tree; church modes are the nails and fastenings. In them is no life, yet they serve life. Growth is the reconcilement of permanence and change. Because of life there is growth; therefore both permanence and change. We give not the life, yet by our good or bad training we hinder or help its fairest and fullest advance." As he thus mused, because of the time and its evils and difficulties, his spirit "wrought, and was tempestuous "with baffled thinkings. He was as a solitary fisherman, tossing in his little boat upon the great sea, spreading out vainly his net of endeavouring thought; his only light, the dim lamp of his own experience.

Thus he now appeared to himself. "But sometimes," thought he, "our state images itself in somewhat another way. The heart seems as a vessel; the mind, the wide-sweeping-net; the world, the full sea. We gather so much that our laden heart begins to sink. Then our cry is, 'I am but man, sinful man, O Lord!' Such an outcry was the book Ecclesiastes, as the great heart felt itself sinking, laden with vast experience of the world. But there comes deliverance, when God brings the heart to its desired haven. The load that well-nigh sank it, then becomes very precious—its exceeding great reward for labour and heaviness."

Presently Theophilus fell into a meditation concerning the great men of the earth, and it arose somewhat thus:—Passing his hand across his forehead, he felt moisture on his brow. "Sweat of the brain," thought he; "how gladly would I sometimes exchange it for the sweat of the arm! Yet many toil with the arm, and the heart, and the mind too. Truly the travail of man is great. There must be hope for man; the world shall have rest from its labours. Perhaps it is good for a world, as for a man, to 'bear the yoke in its youth.' Our hope for self is strongest and least selfish when it is blended with our hope for the world. I seek wisdom; and my endeavour, though often wearying, cannot be in vain. But my chief hope is here; there is wisdom for the world, and of this I may be partaker. Bright doors shall be opened into the inaccessible light, and I may be one of the great entering company."

Big, heavy clouds were now rolling across heaven. These Theophilus saw, and they influenced his meditation. "As for wisdom, the form of its doctrines is very variable. Sometimes for a while steady and majestic, like clouds of a summer sunset; at others, loose, hurrying, and shapeless, like the ragged clouds that now sweep the sky; yet in all forms they bring or announce the nourishing rains. How good was it for the ancients to think of wisdom as a person! And for us the wisdom of God is not just varying doctrines, but a Person who 'abideth for ever.' The Son of God, He is the wisdom of God. For ages, around the memory of this Great One has been the rallying of the world's love and hope. He is that light in the clouds, but above them, which they may obscure but cannot quench; nay, which often dwells in them as in its own glorifying pavilion of beauty, though so far beyond and above them in the deep heavens. And this ' Person,' this heavenly King of wisdom, would want His highest title, ' King of Kings,' were there not many other great and wise ones to whom honour is due. Truly these kings of souls are Heaven's great gifts to men."

A bright star, suddenly beaming out from among the hasty clouds, met Theophilus' eye through the upper panes of his window. "Stars!" thought he, "ye are good emblems of the prophets and great men now afar off 'in the deep backward and abysm of time.' Faint lights the distant stars send us; yet we know that they are very bright, and that around them lesser worlds are floating, dark themselves, but by them illumined. The great spiritual leaders that we see afar off, as if alone, were not alone; around them were many whom God by them comforted and guided. Such men have been centres of love, and truth, and order, possessing energy of gravitation as well as energy of light and heat. Each such man produces harmony in a certain sphere. But how many men have there been of strength indeed, but neither very wise nor good! These have produced orderings, like the orderings of armies for clash and conflict. And so we have innumerable systems of usage and opinion, as in confusions inexplicable, and contentions without issue. Yet a meaning there is, and an issue there is."

The loudness of the wind, that here for a moment disturbed Theophilus, helped forward his meditation. It proceeded thus: " What strife has there ever been in the thoughts and ways of men! What storms! Yet the storms that often precede peace, prepare for it. And there is a law of storms, though we know it not. Who can tell what winds and lightnings do for the mellowing of the fruit? How good is it that we have the history of great souls in whom dark and bright alternated, and in whom fruitfulness and fair weather followed days made sadly changeful with frequent wind and gloom! The remarkable men, and the remarkable times too, are as the magnifying of the common ones. Their histories are as great round disks, upon which we may see our ordinary thoughts and passions largely and clearly presented, and their hidden workings revealed for study. The grander and mightier struggles, yearnings, hopes, and fears, belong to the few; but they represent infinite lesser ones equally real, in the great multitude of men. For common men God cares—they are His people ; and the few, elect not to privilege alone, but to labours, are the officers of His people."

It was now near midnight. Theophilus, weary, threw himself on his chair by the fireside.

The moon had risen high, and the clearing heavens gave promise of at least a bright half-hour. Theophilus rose, put together the embers of his fire, unbarred the door of his garden, his frequent place of evening prayer, and walked forth into the moonlight. The pure, keen air refreshed and exhilarated him. The universe seemed to him a majestic organ ; the heart's emotion, the wind that fills it. The hand of the careful can bring forth harmonies in melodious succession ; but none can worthily exhibit the magnificence and compass of the instrument. Patches of vapour were sailing like little vessels rapidly over the clear sky, some becoming visible as they neared the moon, then radiant, then soon passing again into darkness. As song of accompaniment to the organ-music of heaven, Theophilus fashioned this strain :—

> I saw a cloud
>   Passing the moon ;
> It brighten'd and it darken'd,
>   And vanish'd soon.

It came on my sight
  From the southern heaven;
By one wind into light
  And into darkness driven.

Dimly from the deep
  It uprose on high;
Then it shone far and wide,
  Then it melted in the sky.

Thus it is that man
  Comes to wisdom's noon;
Brightening as this cloud,
  He vanishes as soon.

His beauty is upon him
  While light is given;
Swiftly forward is he speeded
  By the breath of heaven.

From darkness of the deep
  He comes forth on high;
Then in silence he departs—
  But it is into the sky.

It was at another season of the year that Theophilus wrote the Thoughts and the Hymn that
follow :—

NATURE.

Nature, being a book which God has written
out of His heart, contains deep things of His
heart. The better reader it has, and the more

he ponders it, the more does it teach him and
the more does it move him. The teaching and
the moving are distinguishable, though more
and more will they be at one, mutually helpful.
The love of God dwells in and with the mind of
God; they are eternally distinct, yet eternally
co-inherent. And in man the gradually com-
pleting, and but now, as it were, sketched or
roughly moulded image of God; feeling and
thought, not alone distinct, but too often
opposed, are more and more to be manifested
in unity. Nature is the work of God in the
fulness of His being. Creation was heart-work,
and not alone mind-work—and so there is in
the things and appearances of the world, their
order and variousness, adaptation to the spirit
of man. As heart answers to heart, so surely
answers the heart of man, beholding the world,
to the heart of God who made it. But it is as
man's heart becomes like God's, that he more
sees and feels in the Divine work what God
Himself does. And so nature, the world visible,
becomes more the satisfying exponent of the
purpose, thought, and goodness of the King
invisible. Yet is nature insufficient for the esta-
blishment and maintenance of what alone can
be justly called a humanly natural religion.

Revealed religion, in which God shows Himself as man—man working, suffering, and succeeding—can alone witness itself as truly our natural religion, religion according to our nature and wants. " Natural religion " commonly means religion that the visible world can originate and nourish—give now, and give alone. So the world is made to say, "Receive me, not Christ: I will suffice thee." But things visible are insufficient; in part because of our imperfection, in part because of their own incompleteness. They are a writing of Divine, true sayings ; but not of all the Divine, true sayings. They teach not all, nor teach their own word fully without other teaching. For Messiah says, " Receive Me, and have the world also. It shall now do all its work for thee better, for I will strengthen it." Reading of ourself in one like ourself, as we become more truly human the world becomes to us more truly Divine. But Divine in itself it ever is—and much Divine influence it ever has, whether Christ be known or not known. The love of nature is a help to holiness. Revive within those who have wrought folly, the remembrance of sounds and scenes in which they delighted with innocent delight, and you show them that they have been with God, and God with them. The awakened grieving, but loving remembrance of dead innocence, may urge to prayer and purpose of heart concerning the holy. Holiness is the regeneration of innocence. Fair but perishable innocence dies. God can bring it again from the dead, as a spirit made "perfect;" for holiness is innocence made perfect. For the "wise of heart," who have turned from folly, there is joy and strength in contemplative beholding, in sport and musing, genial hours of mirth or devotion amidst natural scenes. Cattle in the pastures—the soft darkness of clear distances beyond these pastures—the broad, bright, unhidden spaces of deep blue above—the stately, calm-sweeping clouds, voluminously built up like ship-palaces of the sky, limited off from the broad expanse of heaven by bright gold margins;—as we behold these, the spirit exults weepingly—has at once within it strange swellings and repose,—feels holy love, and devout, heavenly longing quite inexpressible—feels as in God, and as having God with it. And most truly is it so; for now is there communion of the creating and the created heart. There is silence. Deep is the joy of social silence when we speak not with the loved, but feel their presence. And now, in this our silence, is there consciousness of highest intercourse. We are wrapt into the grandest of the social sympathies; that with Him whose we are, and from whom our love is. All present heavenliness of temper in a world much confused by vexing changes, gives us anticipation and glimpse of that to which we are redeemed—that betterness of spirit and estate. Neither the Redeemer nor redeeming love can be apprehended with any sufficiency and answering love by man, unless he hopefully long for the eternal life, because of his present joy in present sorrow—the earnest of its full possession, and the proof of kindred life already within us. As gold given for earnest of gold, so is life given for earnest of life. Natural beauty works on us as a breathing of life from God. He who, walking in his garden, meditates Christ's appearing, course of life, and dying, that he may experience devout thankfulness, aspiration, and satisfying quiet of reason, may have aid of the Divine Spirit, a breathing from God upon him, through his beholding of some lesser and familiar instance of creative kindness. He may see, under the eaves of his house, the bird visiting her young with nourishment. Sedulously she continues her labour of love, joyously is she received at each return. This near instance of

D

the love of God may cause the man to glow with a loving temper—may give him "comfort of love," that enables him with a freshened spirit to consider the great things on which he meditates—nay, may cause to arise within him a mist-dispersing wind; so that now, through a clear atmosphere, he discerns the breadth of the Christian country, and all its variety of objects, whilst freely down upon him from above are poured the life-quickening, beauty-spreading beams of the sun. The more holy the man, the more has the world to him a "beauty of holiness," and a wisdom of holiness. It is holy; for God is, and He made it.

HYMN AT EVENING.

I sat at evening in the shade,
   A Bible on my knee;
Still heaven beautiful above,
   Cool air around me free.

And thoughts upon my spirit moved,
   Stirr'd by the evening's charm,
Softly as clouds that floated by
   Upon the heaven calm.

And turning Godward, every thought
   Found beauty and a rest,
As grey clouds sunward travelling
   Grow golden in the west.

Then like the Maker seem'd His work,
   So beautiful, so strong;
As grand as old eternity—
   Pure as a maiden young.

Man's early love, the earth and heavens,
   Has charms that cannot tire;
Beauty in movement and in rest—
   What change would we desire?

Oh! who is he would wish the stars
   New-scatter'd in the sky—
No more Orion and the Bear
   On winter night to spy?

Who would new vest the green-robed earth
   Or crave of Heaven, as boon,
A bluer sky, a brighter sun,
   Or a serener moon?

While tiny-handed little ones
   Are fashioning a bower,
Age with his sorrow-whiten'd head
   Stoops to a budding flower.

Then said my heart, " This word of Christ,
   The word of love and truth,
Is fresh and sweet to young and old,
   For in itself is youth.

The story is a deep-cupp'd flower,
   Of richest inward dye;
The truths are as the midnight stars,
   That speak immensity;

And He, an ever-beaming sun,
　Whose beauty and whose might,
Red-rising from its cloudy dawn,
　Makes a creation bright.

So, Lord, Thy Word, even as Thy work,
　We love until we die;
And added truth and wonder fresh
　Thou wilt disclose on high."

CHAPTER III.

MORNING! morning! first a glimmer, then a glow, and then the giant of the skies comes forth, his face freshly bright, because his heart is in his great work of lighting the nations.

> Again I wake,
>   O living One! in Thee
>   Newly I am, and move:
> Wilt Thou not make
>   My heart a garden be.
>   Thy presence unto me
> Soft, sunny air of love?
>
> Forth shall I go,
>   Pursuing without fear
>   My work of life begun;
> If Thee I know
>   As great, yet very dear,
>   Far off, but very near,
> A sunshine and a Sun.

The world wakes, and I wake. I step out into the companionable sunshine—look towards

the sun, so mighty and so distant—and make
my little hymn my prayer, not to the great light
of the earth and heavens, but to Him whose
work and whose witness that great light is.

The night, dark and silent, and cold and
lonely, is gone: many watchers for the morning
are satisfied. Is not the history of the world
as a watching for the morning? To Him who
regardeth a thousand years as a day, they are
also but as a watch in the night; and His is a
watching that shall not fail. In one view, the
course of the world, from its beginning to its
ending, is as a course of many days; in another,
it is as one great night, and the ages are the
night-watches. The morning shall interpret.
The darkness of the times that now are, is as
the dark womb of the times of new earth and
heavens that shall be. Strange are the trans-
ition shapes of organisms; but for the foreseen
perfect shapes are they preparations. In the
Divine Book all the members of the earth are
written which in continuance shall be fashioned.
He who taketh up the isles as a very little thing,
accounteth of a thousand years as a very
little time. But can we so account them? In
one sense, no; in another, yes. We are
"children" of God; and as a child cannot

exercise a man's patience, our waiting must be according to our childly feeling and capacity. Human patience cannot be as Divine. But the wise teacher becomes as the child in part, that in part he may cause the child to become as himself. And the courses of our life and of the world's are so ordered by the great Trainer of men, that we shall have a joy and success after a waiting and endeavour proportioned to our strength as men, and yet shall be drawn more and more into sympathy with the vast views of our Maker. The Christian who is patient with himself and with men, shall not spend strength for nought; yet neither shall he, nor those that are with him, hastily or perfectly make the world as they would see it. Christ is the chief "husbandman" of the earth, who has "long patience;" and Christianity is but doing its second day's work. The second thousand years are not ended.

Theophilus loved the morning; yet he rose not early. In first years he had done so, and he hoped again to do so in later years; but in his student days it was not possible as a habit. Yet, though he saw not usually the sun rise, he was astir soon enough to feel the freshness of the young day's life. It was, he said, illus-

trative of his catholicity, that he had such cordial regard for a creature of habits so foreign
to his own as the lark.   But, said he, the bird
and I have truly agreement at heart; and ever
this is the just catholicity—that diversities hinder
not friendship, because of deep inward ground of
agreement.

Walking in his garden earlier than usual, on a
morning brighter than usual, and gazing fixedly,
in, "love and joy and peace," at blooms, bathed
as seemed to him in the pure light ; in the following poem, he uttered the morning thought
of his heart that rose :—

SUNSHINE.

At sunny morning, when the eye
  Is on a plant directed,
Not only from each bloom and leaf
  A soft light is reflected;
The space between the eye and flower
  The sunshine seems to fill,
As if the light a water were,
  Lying very clear and still.

The form-full world so various,
   In light-full air reposes,
And in the fresh-flowing sunshine bathed,
   Each form its grace discloses;
And thus the wonder-world of Truth
   Its myriad forms doth show,
When fresh its fairer light of Love
   From God its sun doth flow.

Our thought it is the air; and when
   Our mind its eye directeth,
At dawn of love, upon some truth,
   What soft light it reflecteth!
And not alone the truth we see,
   In fairness doth appear,
But Love which brightens, shows itself
   All sunny-rich, and clear.

OTHER MORNING THOUGHTS, WITH
A MORNING POEM.

"There be many that say, Who will
show us any good?" "We will," reply "all
Seasons and their change." "I will," says the
Morning; "when I come forth with face shining
as if fresh from the presence of God, I have
healthy breezes and pleasant songs." "And I
will," says the Evening; "when with serious joy
I go away into the darkness as one returning to

God, to rest with Him, and bring to Him my
works.   My heavens, serene and sublime, shall
be over thee as His wing." "And I will," says
the Summer; "I am fruitful and happy and
rich." "And I will," says the Winter; "I have
beauty of the snow, and cheerfulness of home
fires."   Shall man answer: "Miserable com-
forters are ye all!" saying to the Morning,
"Thou singest songs to a heavy heart;" and to
the Evening, "Thou sayest, Peace, peace, when
there is no peace;" to the Summer, "When
we desire thy fruits, they may not be ours, and
when they fall to us, appetite is gone;" and to
the Winter, "Who can heed beauty of the snow
in the freezing wind? and what to us are thy
fires, when the heart within us is desolate?"

Oftentimes, when men have been ready
thus to speak, they have been gently overpowered.   They have been charmed into hope
and into healing.   The angel of content has
won over them a mild victory with a touch, and
they have softened into peace. In the "seasons
and their change," and in the best religious
books, usages, and remembrances, there is
charmlike influence.   The good angels first
speak to us, and we rebut their words; but
they are near us, and touch us, and then, in

spite of ourselves, we are gently overpowered, and our vexed mood is quieted. And these Strengths, that heal us when sick, increase our joy of health when well. We are kindly shamed too, as by a friend's look, when such blessing of peace and cheerfulness comes to us in our discontents. We must needs give thanks, if not in word, yet with our heart, for the blessing; but a little while ago, we were ready even to curse. Why so hasty? did we well to be angry? If such a sweet delivering cheerfulness comes to us in the morning, it is like the dew on the flowers,—

THOUGH TRANSIENT, NOT VAIN.

At early morning, on a flower
   A dewdrop rested, large and cool;
The sun arose, and in an hour
   The blossom open'd fair and full:
But the dewdrop, child of dawn and night,
Erewhile rejoicing in the light,
Already it had vanish'd quite.

At early morning, on a heart
   Joy rested, pure, and fresh, and still;
The world awoke, and part by part
   Unfolded strength, and thought, and will:
But the joy, the child of night and dawn,
One hour but pass'd since it was born,
Brief-lived, it had already gone.

But the noon came, and heart and flower
    Fronted the light, each strong and fair,
Nor dew nor joy in one short hour
    Breathed forth a vain life to the air;
From each an offering rose to heaven,
By each true nourishment was given,
And thus both man and plant have thriven.

"We feel most," said Theophilus, "the sweetness and the sacredness of good, when, coming, it at once relieves from the worst, hints to us the better, and gives to us a present healthy glow."   Then brightens—

THE SKY OF OUR HEART.

Oh! how soft and exquisite,
    On a morning vapoury,
      When the weather clears
    After long, dark rain,
Is the blue behind the white
    And delicate mist-drapery,
      In which the sky appears
    Attired again ;
And cloud-robed heaven in the windiness
Shows like a lady beautiful in her undress !

It is the rain the heaven clears;
   Then the pure blue, pale
      Or deep, in glimpse is seen
   The clouds above:
So the heart is brighter for its tears,
   And return of peace we hail,
      Showing as if between
   Words of hope and love:
Then how beautiful the spirit is in this undress—
The mild heart-utterance of uncarefulness!

THE PARTIAL AND TRANSIENT.

The same day will, to different persons, at different places, distribute rain and drought, thick mists and fair blue sky. At every moment beauty is seen and bounty enjoyed somewhere; and at every moment a like reality have gloom and grief. But where there is bright weather now, there will be rain presently; and where the rain falls now, there will be clear shining soon. And often just where the clouds are, the fields are becoming greener; but where the blue sky is, the earth remains parched and dry. So then, we may say, If a man would have his spirit as a productive garden, he must be content sometimes to lose for a while sunshine and brightness, though these he will cer-

tainly need, and these he may desire and hope
for.   But our own garden is not our people's
country, nor is either our spirit or our country
the world.   The world falls not into a sadness
because we are melancholy; and when we are
receiving our pleasant things, many are in un-
comforted sorrow.   But the world often for us
takes hue and aspect from the predominant
state of our spirit; it seems summerly or win-
terly, dark or bright, according to the change
of our inward times and seasons.   We breathe
upon it the summer power or winter power
that makes it seem as we are.   Now, while the
merry heart certainly may make the cheerful
countenance, and he who is sad, allowably may
weep—we should yet ever recognize as we can
what is real in itself and for others, when not
real for us; and deal equitably in our thought
between opposites of heart-state and condition.
Wonderful is it how God causes, and at the
same hour has sympathy with, both the dark
and bright!   Can there be but one supreme
heart over the world, when at the same moment
mildly sounds the brook in the meadow, and
hoarsely rage the destructive sea waves?   There
is but one great heart; then how wonderful
a heart!   While hundreds die on the battle-

field in agony and horror, over a thousand spots the sun is shining, and the birds sing. God beholds all. The fire that in slow torture consumes the martyr, from His air gains intensity; and at these same moments this same air refreshes and exhilarates myriads of happy beings. He has sympathy for the sufferer; yet does He not withhold joy from those for whom, according to His own wonderful order, it is now fitting. He has sympathy for these also. One man is on the rack, another in the dance, and the nerves of each have their thrill of pain or delight because of the operation of the Divine natural law. Let us not so think of city lanes as to forget country valleys, nor so please ourselves with instruments of music as to disregard the voice of misery. We are ever viewing things too narrowly. We speak, for example, of certain times as times of crisis, when we are but considering this or the other interest. There may be a crisis for a class, while the great interests of the people are safe; a crisis for a people, while those of the world are secure; and a crisis for a man's fortunes, while God takes most careful charge of his spirit. Ten miles to the north of a great city, a hail-storm may destroy some ripening wheat-

field, while over the great city is outstretched
a bright, still heaven. There will be some
sheaves less of corn, but the traffic of the
corn-market will proceed. The great laws of
the world are ever steadily prevailing, and
even when Truth and Good stand before us as
trees in winter, without foliage or sign of life,
they are but quietly invigorating their vitality,
preparing to put forth, in new abundance, fruits
for the joy and healing of the nations. The
individual may not have peace till he feels
that his good is the good of the many, and
the good of the many his own; his evil also
for the good of the many, and their evil for
the good of the world, and hence for his.

These words concerning the partial and transient, will, by their last sentence, serve well
to introduce some kindred ones on the individual; but we interpose two poems. The first
was the child of a winter day; the second
was born in one of the grand summer storms
of rain and wind.

DEPENDENCE.

Is there a lily or a thought
  That in thy heart or garden grows?
By patient carefulness and skill
  Each into beauty rose;
But alike the lily and the thought
  Has life, that from the Maker flows.

Knowest thou not that dim and bare
  Thy spirit garden may become;
And for the sun-loved summer bright,
  With peacefulness and bloom,
Be darkening and heavy mists,
  Winter rigidity and gloom?

Know also that creating God
  Rules every life as every land;
A spirit-energizing power
  Goes forth at His command;
That thought may bloom, desire breathe,
  Delight as opening heaven stand.

When pass thy Joys as summer flowers,
  Thy Being endures as winter tree,
Which sleeps disrobed, dreaming of growth,
  That shall enlarged be,
When Time, the low-fallen winter sun,
  Ascends again revivingly.

CHANGE.

Loud winds bluster,
  The long rains fall;
Yet ripen'd fruits will cluster
  Upon tree and wall;
For wind and darkness passing,
  Come flowers and perfume;
And in peace and light that follow
  Open foliage and bloom;
Then the corn to full ear, fruit to ripeness,
  In order due shall come.

Gusts howl and sweep,
  The bitter waters foam;
Yet the mariners on the deep
  Shall rest in their home;
For the blue of ocean and of air
  Will both again be bright,
And waves and stars will sparkle
  In the cool, still night;
And steady winds blowing,
  Bring the shore in sight.

Big clouds darken,
  The lightnings shoot;
Yet again shall we hearken
  To the birds' glad note;
For the heavy drops fallen,
  The hidden sun will beam;

The clouds will melt and vanish,
　The golden light will stream,
And the freshen'd earth with fragrance
　And melody will teem.

All change changing,
　Works and brings good ;
And though frequent storms, ranging;
　Carry fire and flood ;
And the growing corn is beaten down,
　The young fruits fall and moulder,
The vessels reel, the mariners drown,
　Awing the beholder;
Yet in evil to men is good for man,
　Then let our heart be bolder ;
For more and more shall appear the plan,
　As the world and we grow older.

THE INDIVIDUAL.

The whole loves its parts. It alone has
excellent glory as they have finish and beauty,
possess their forms, and fill their places. Birds
and dewdrops are perfect in their kind; and
for them the sun shines. The modest, unnoticed
goodness of unknown men and women reveals
the great God, and honours Him; and for such
Christ lived and died. As hours of Sabbath

worship pass, the world moves on in its course many thousands of miles; but also in the quiet fields small flowers open to the light. The sun controls the movement of the world, and of many worlds, yet lifts the head of each flower, brightens its face, and unfolds all its blossoming. The orb Truth gladdens the heart of many a worshipper, lifts it, brightens it; yet this orb has forces which the great spiritual world in all its onward movements must obey. How beautifully is a bud folded! how perfect a snow-flake! What is a bud in a forest? yet is it beautiful as if alone. What is one snow-flake of the mantle that wraps the mountain-top? yet is it perfect as if alone, and reflects part of the early golden light of the advancing sun. Each man is a man, and may have his individuality of work and worth. A good man among the good, is as one of the drops on which God paints the rainbow; for good men are to the world its rainbow of Divine promise and hope; and the goodness of no man is lost. Every raindrop does its part in dissolving light into colour; and though we may seem to ourselves like those drops which, falling near our window, make to us no part of the bow, yet we too have our brightness and place, forming part of the arch as seen by some

—that arch which "the hands of the Most High have bended." And not only has the individual good man ever due place among the many : at times his individual goodness may have a worth quite special. One man of pure, and merciful, and patient life, shall at times better represent God to us than shall the Church, or what by us is so named; even as on a drop of morning dew, lying calm and still, a more perfect image of the sun appears than on the vast sea distracted by tumultuous winds. On the sea there is a wide-diffused lustre; but on the dewdrop a serene, clear brightness. We, and our work, and our history, all have worth, and may have special worth. If we understand not the great movements by which we with the world are borne onward, shall it give us no joy that these are ruled by a law of wise beneficence? If we know not how our work of life shall interweave with other work of life for the good of the world, shall it not delight us that thus it is ordered? As we stand in evening silence, and listen to the hum of some great city, it is no articulate voice of intelligence that we hear; yet what almost infinite fulness of intelligence does the sound represent! It is from a sea of living spirits that this great tide of sound rolls forth ;

and we may rejoice to hear such a voice from the great deep of life, though we understand it not. True is it, that groans and curses, the noise of much evil work and utterance, are in the voice, though we hear not these. But the wide, still, evening heaven serves to us as emblem of that serene, composed intelligence which ever has rest in consciousness of wisdom, which sees order in confusion, good in evil, even now, and shall hereafter make these gloriously appear. Our work and our utterance may make to others but part of the loud sounding of a living people; yet is there for us, and for each man, a Divine eye and ear. We are not lost in the multitude; we too may live for a worthy end. We may honour our Maker, and benefit our race.

These few lines on the Future will perhaps suitably close this chapter :—

THE FUTURE.

Founded upon the cloudy dark,
  God builds a palace bright,
And many watching spirits mark
  Its progress with delight :
But thinnest mists of curtaining Time
  Conceal from man the sight ;
Although the lofty pillars are
  Of coruscating light :

So many and so fair as those
   That fill the northern night,
Upstretching from the horizon's verge
   Even to the zenith's height :
And this shall be the home of man,
   When it is finish'd quite,
If that he now endure and work,
   So spending life aright.

CHAPTER IV.

EXTRACTS FROM A JOURNAL.

HEAVINESS in the heart of man causeth it to stoop, but a good word maketh it glad. There is a good word concerning heaviness itself, that may make glad; this, namely, that the heart is the productive tree, and its heaviness may be that of the fruity boughs of thought, laden with the weight of their ripening fruits. But if we be heavy because of waiting for success, this is the lesson for us—that early successes are mostly rather according to wish than wisdom. We take show for good—deceived by a vain show, because it is a fine one; so we get confirmed love for the showy and the immediate, and are neither in our works nor ways conscious partakers of a Divine everlastingness. If our garden be small, then let us fill it with choice flowers;

and such a love of choice things shall we form in ourselves, that if a larger garden be given us, it will be worthily filled. To do well, is to do choicely. And if a man keep the house in order over which he has charge, small though it be, he shall have Divine comforts. These shall have light and beauty for him in sad hours—as, in the dusk of evening, white flowers shine brightly through the shade, and seem pure and sacred. Many fair colours are now hidden; but these white blooms, that have blossomed from the roots of pious thoughts and acts, beam to cheer and hallow the dusk. Not alone, however, we say, If the things we have be few, let them be choice; but also say, Let us not too readily cry, in haste or peevishness, that the things we can do or can have are few : let us collect these in our thought; then, perhaps, we may seem to ourselves to be—

POOR, YET POSSESSING.

Thy garden may seem poor and small,
  Of flowers scanty the supply;
But go and gather them, and then
  The blossom-bunch shows handsomely.
Sweet and many are they found,
  These the products of thy ground.

Thoughts and fancies that arise
  Beautiful and true ;
Actions serviceable, kind,
  In our power to do ;
Gifts and mercies we receive
  May scanty seem and few ;
But, gathering them, we find
    Something we. have and something are.
      Poor they look dispersed ;
      Cluster'd, very fair.
And this wealth we may increase
  By diligence and care.
Hope is born of thankfulness ;
  But of palsying despair
Thou the ready victim art,
Viewing good things but apart.

———————

Across a stream there runs a slender quivering bridge. A tree grows near, overhanging the waters. You can reach the boughs, and seizing but a twig, it will serve to steady you in your passage of the stream. Time and each day is the stream; perhaps a stream eddying and sounding. The Divine word of wisdom is the tree. By the narrow quivering bridge of obedience may you make a safe though perhaps a trembling passage, if you seize and hold one of those living branches of the tree that are bending towards you.

A man may from a hill see clearly the house or spot in the distance towards which he intends to journey; he may see also the winding road that will lead him thither; and yet when he descends the hill for travel he may lose his way, and may be long puzzled which road to take. He may have to reascend new hills as he advances, and to make inquiries again and again. We look forward from the hill of Consideration, but we travel over the intricate valley country of Experiment. We shall go quite wrong, and become over-weary and discouraged, unless we seek and gladly accept kind hints of guidance from those around us, and often repeat our partial surveys of the ground we traverse. Here, then, are lessons concerning trust and knowledge in the way of life. For trust we must obey, as depending; for knowledge we must consider and inquire. Old lessons these, yet needed.

If we say to a thing, Are you possible? the answer is, Try. Few things seem so possible as they are till they are attempted. Till we have decisively made attempts, we neither have for work full heart nor full power.

> Thoughts of work without attempting
>   Bring moodiness and despair;
> For a man may swim in the waters,
>   But he cannot swim in air.

He may drown in the waters, but at least he cannot swim out of them. Thrice blessed, then, is Necessity, that servant of God and friend of man, which, when action is needed, but heart wanting, casts us forth as birds from our nests! As we unfold our wings we find that we have power to fly, and they strength to sustain us. He who regards the written or spoken experience of men has Wisdom, as the old eagle, to take him at first and bear him on her wing; or as an old seaman, who, throwing him into the waters, stands near to help, that he perish not in his struggles to swim. In walking, we stagger onward to stability; in writing, at first we slowly make unshapely marks, but at last we swiftly form characters fair and regular. Ever we begin attempt without full power to perform. It is as if the arm lengthened as it extended itself to pluck the fruit. Neither our own power nor the world's help can we know without trial. When the wind blows against the current of a river, if we fix the eye on the waters they shall seem to obey the wind and flow backward. But if we cast in straws or wood we shall see soon that the waves mock us with a semblance. The winds cannot keep the rivers from the sea. They may vex us, but the currents will help us. The world has its slope, and the flow of waters finally obeys it. We must judge the course of the streams of things not by a gaze, but by a venture, and then trust the permanent set of the current. In the course of our endeavours, our own forces, and the provided helps of the course of things, will more and more reveal themselves. It will be we, but not we alone. To the artist, as he feels more his own life and power in his works, nature becomes more admirable and wonderful: so is it with all endeavour. The good worker makes this his motto in working: "God for us: God with us." Every success, improving faculty, increases confidence. The addition of power becomes a factor in relation to an indefinite number of efforts and modes of effort; and the confidence is one that finds in each experienced success a guarantee for new combinations of assistances.

In practicalness, we require honesty to do something; wisdom to do the thing possible,

and next us; courage to do poorly, and as at
our worst, when we must do this or nothing.
We can only, then, satisfactorily affirm to ourselves the dominance of a spiritual affection,
when conscious of an answering practical
tendency. There must be a confidential friend-
liness between our moral meditation and our
common conduct, else we despise self, and
others will despise us; we become moralizing
liars to ourselves, and our resolution neither to
self nor others vouches for a deed. Often we
will not plant our acorn, because it springs not
up at once before our eyes an oak. We feel that
in a manner we have the grown oak within us;
can see it, but cannot show it. Our vision
deceives us not, if as a vision we regard it; it is
a true dream of prophecy. A stout oak for
timber and for shelter there may rise; but, as
yet, it is not except in vision. We must plant
our germ in the soil Fact, and be patient, for the
first shoots will be feeble, and the growth slow.
The thinking man has wings; the acting man
has only feet and hands. It is what the hand
findeth to do that must be done with might;
and what the hand findeth, must be at hand—
reachable. The eye pierces into infinite space;
so is it with man's thought and hope. The hand

reaches forward but a yard; so is it with man's
work: it is where he is that man must labour.
In our deed, we must not so much be afraid of
bungling and inadequacy, as beware of in-
sincerity. He who persists in genuineness will
increase in adequacy. Pride frustrates its own
desire; it will not mount the steps of the throne,
because it has not yet the crown on. But till
first throned we may not be crowned. Pride
would be acknowledged victor before it has won
the battle. It will not act, unless it be allowed
that it can succeed; and it will do nothing
rather than not do brilliantly. It is well sometimes to fall below self—sometimes to fail. Not
only thus are we goaded and stirred, and our
resolve braced; but the effort being one that
conscience demanded, saying, Do what you can,
we get assurance that we love excellence, and
not alone have complacency in our own mani-
festations of ability. A Divine blessing is on
industry according to forethought—on a step-by-
step advance according to tentative, approxima-
tive method. It is thus we gain success, inward
and in the world; it is thus that we come to
the heights and hidden places where Truth has
inscribed words, erected memorials of things
done, or prepared stations for outlook upon

extensive prospects ; it is thus that we obtain place and influence amongst men, clear some little space in the wilderness of the world, and leave behind us timber-trees and fruit-trees in its forests and orchards.

The arm and the hand tremble after much labour or the carriage of heavy weights ; is, then, the hand no longer skilful, nor the arm strong ? Still may we truly so account them, because of the powers of the living frame that will revive them. The mind and the heart may tremble after meditations and experiences ; they cannot fix themselves for steady, composed behaviour, or for steady, contemplative, examining thought : yet still the heart may be a "good heart," and the mind bright and powerful. From the reservoir of life shall they be resupplied and invigorated. Our spirits are wells of water, which, from much drawing, may become dry ; yet will they certainly refill, because of streams that ooze or flow into them continually. Because of the " chances and changes of this mortal life,". there are often departures and returns of our inward states of joy and faith. When we have learned that joy and faith are worked for, yet bestowed—then, because they are so much *gifts*,

though we may have lost hope of their reat-
tainment, we need not abandon hope of their
repossession. The good heart, the glad heart
and the trusting, is "in deaths oft;" yet is it
" alive again." Our faith "was lost;" yet is
it again " found." Sometimes the returns of
old feelings of devoutness or peace come with
such freshness of strength, that they are like
the returns of those who went from us but to
seek health, and the bloom of whose countenance, when they come back, shows that they
have sought it successfully. And the remembrance of such a return is as that of a visit from
one with a heart like our own, yet brighter—
who brightened ours, and has left us the thought
of him as a protective charm against the evil
spirits of doubt and fear that we may meet with
in dark, lonely places.

F

TRUST.

The truth that thou dost Feel to-day,
  Thou mayest only Know to-morrow;
Love with thy joy may pass away,
  And doubt may come with sorrow.

Then thou with Truth affronted art;
  Yet wilt thou say, when sorrows heal,
From confidence why did I part ?—
  Behold, again I Feel !

Then loving much, as one forgiven,
  Thou believest Truth, thy present friend;
Saying, I will serve and trust thee even
  Until my life shall end.

But thou in change again wilt fail—
  Doubting again, and angry be ;
Then comforted, thy fault bewail
  In sad humility.

More is thy friend than what he gives,
  Though by his gift his heart he proves
And thou must learn, The absent lives,
  And unforgetting loves.

In confidence hold on thy way,
  Patient endure the allotted sorrow;
The truth is Known to thee to-day—
  It will be Felt to-morrow.

Let man do what he will, exercise himself, store himself, fortify himself, there shall be much frustration and surprise; he shall be made to feel that it is not in himself to determine wholly what shall come upon him and be felt within him—made to feel this, perhaps, to his vexation and distrust, though afterward taught to say gratefully, It was well. The ends we purpose may be good, our means selected, wise; but neither can we, by our own effort, nor the aid of others, be so instructed and strengthened as to pursue and attain surely, according to our thought. There will be, at one time or another, interferences of unusual event, to break the spiritually lethargizing influence of an anticipated usualness; not alone to remind us that God is and acts, but to teach us how dull and inadequate is our thought of His being and acting. Moral truths are prophecies of ends, but not of the forms and succession of events. Unanticipated and unpredictable good and evil will both occur. Of the evil, hinderance which is yet not hinderance, this is a sanative and strengthening thought; that as a wise man, if wiser, would deal with himself, so the Divine Providence deals with him. A wise man will submit himself to many disciplines, if he clearly sees their necessity and advantage, from which, if less spiritually advanced, he would shrink, and which, if then imposed on him, he would regard as hardship and injustice. The advance of our nature is anticipated for us, and we are so placed and treated, as, if wiser and of a more stedfast will, we should voluntarily place and treat ourselves. Much seems to us wrong at the time; but afterwards we vindicate the wisdom we mistrusted, and former doubt strengthens present confidence.

The unpredictable and unhoped good often comes just in time to save from fainting; it interprets the past, shows a preparation made for its own coming, and reveals a bounty greater than we dared believe to be. Thus, to-day's work may be followed by to-morrow's unhappiness; and the third day's joy no way originating from the unhappiness, yet only possible through it, may show that in our work there was great reward. As in geometry so in life, distinct threads of influencing truth are often introduced abruptly, presently to be interwoven with one or with several of the many-threaded and related lines of truth. When the good comes, then we know that just the different knowledges needed, or the qualities of character most serviceable, have been imparted. Thus, because in sustained activity moral endurance and firmly-settled thoughts are necessary, men are for a long time hidden or thwarted, that they may be prepared to act. By, as seems, the too monotonous and too long-continued exercises of a private or confined life, they are prepared for the decisive and powerful performances of a freer and a wider one ; and stepping forth from their narrow prisoning circle, they find that they have a shaping thought by which to build their structure of activities, and that their faculty of endurance is as a massive foundation on which it may be reared. The world is a school in which we are training for character; and we learn severally, as of such tutors as Duty, Order, Beauty, Love, Sorrow, Joy, Labour. We are dominantly for a while under the influence of some one tutor ; but the end of our training is not forgotten, and if we be heedful scholars we shall surely at last be thankful ones.

To these selected extracts we will now add some meditative memoranda on " Our Course in Life," and then close the chapter with some verse on " Wisdom."

OUR COURSE IN LIFE.

We are not in life as on some stream in a boat without oar or sail, gliding smoothly or borne on roughly, as the waters chance to flow. Strength and skill are available ; yet are there ever currents by which our motion is affected. Sometimes we appear as in a labyrinth of disparted streams. Wisdom to choose our course is needful, and much care required at the turnings. The heedless and feeble are often overset, or drifted into dangerous channels ; and sometimes may be seen wrecked vessels borne rapidly by strong currents to a waste of waters, tumultuous amidst rocks and darkness. Fruitless seem struggles for renewed safety—fruitless, efforts to render help. These disasters are partly of fault and partly of fate ; fate being the name men give to supreme will when they know it not as wisdom. Often, again, in his course of life, man feels as a feathered seed driven by winds. As if without weight or power, he slowly floats or is swiftly hurried, but rests nowhere. He feels that within him is life, but knows that he is as yet an embryo. He is confusedly conscious of what his tendencies are, but cannot tell what his outgrowth will be. He floats solitarily among the great trees, and over the expanse of vegetation. Often is he stirred by inward sympathy with the growths around him. Let him but find resting-place, and he also will put forth buds and boughs, and array himself in beauty. Perhaps he shall be driven into the great sea, and his life perish. Is not life given that there may be growth? When shall he, then, find place, and put forth roots and branches? Again, our course in life is often as that of a traveller upon a dark waste scattered over with lamps. A while in the light, we are then in shadow; and so light and gloom alternate as we pass from lamp to lamp. When, resting, we look forward into the future, the knowledge we have serves such use as the distant lamp does. There is a definite point of light surrounded with an indefinite and perhaps hazy luminousness. We see the lamp, but discern not what surrounds; yet it affords us a guiding light, and as we approach it, it will brighten, casting upon our steps a useful glimmer.

As we consider the future—what we shall become, and what will befall us—we mostly form for ourselves a certain ideal both of our lot and of our character. Spiritual men are those who give more earnest heed to what they shall

be and shall do, than to what they shall possess
and enjoy.   But even spiritual men will find it
hard to work cheerfully by day if they have not
a pillow for the night, and to plan useful travels
if they cannot obtain a tent to shelter them in
their wanderings.   To spiritual men, character
will be to condition as soul to body; but if we
have an earnest and predominant regard for
excellence, we shall yet conceive ourselves as
manifesting such excellence in some fit kind of
activity, some suited way of life.   It may seem
to us as if we could alone be of the character
and spirit desired, in some supposed conditions,
and with some supposed opportunities.   The
" body " we thus judge fit for our personality
may be but one stout and vigorous, yet is it
chosen because of a correspondence to the
" soul " that needs it.   It is well that we thus
connect a certain outward life with a particular
inward one.   Outward things thus become spiritual to us, and possess beauty, worth, and en-
dearment, because in and by them we may
exercise spiritual strength and affection.   But if
outward things have thus, though subordinate,
worth; yet, because subordinate, they will admit
of much variation, and still serve spiritual ends.
A strong and beautiful soul will show itself such,

though its body be feeble, sick, or ungraceful.
It is certain that no hungering or penury of our
individual nature is contemptuously disregarded.
Many of our wishes have been, and will be,
thwarted; but repression is not destruction.
Retardation is for the filling in and more perfect
effect of the harmony. The subordination of
the several parts in succession is for the co-
ordination of them all in the perfected man.
Sorrow is surgery. This is the truth for us—
that unless we deliver ourselves to God, He
delivers us to destiny. Destiny is the word for
the Divine *will* not known as such, only known
as power; and often must it be felt as a power
alike loveless and tremendous. By obeying and
enduring, we may rise into knowledge of, and
sympathy with, the *will* that is also wisdom and
love. But foolish and wise must submit alike to
the *will* as power; and to the foolish it is
grievous, and seems tyrannic. That belief in
God, as over all and working in all, which is to
bring us repose and delight, may in early times
make us acquainted with peculiar pains; for to
affirm to ourselves that there is an infinite creating and presiding Love—to hunger for a felt
relationship to Him who, we say, is this love—
to thirst for a partaking of that joy which flows

from Him as His life—and yet to feel as if left
in a dreary solitude darkened with clouds, exposed to bleak winds of destiny without succour
or support;—this is to know bitterness, as of
affection disappointed, love unreturned.   But,
advancing in our course of life with a strenuous
patience, soon the heavenly gates of eternal
Wisdom are seen to lift up their bright heads
before us; and through these we enter with joy
and a song into our rest of faith.

To learn the love of God, is to pass through
dark caverned places as we ascend the hills to
behold sunrise from their tops.   In our journey-
ing, the light was dim, the heights were hidden;
but now we see, and are satisfied.   It is also to
swim through strong waves to a sheltering
island.   When landed, we have joy; but, though
safe in the midst of the "mighty waters," we yet
gaze on them with wonder and awe.   If we
know God truly, we shall say, " How great a
God!"—even when, from our heart's fulness, we
add, " How good! how wise!"

WISDOM.

I sigh,
And while I am musing—
Wishing, but not choosing—
The hours pass by.

Time! Time!
Why is life so brief?
The world is a tree,
Man but a leaf,
So the world flourishes—
But man dies.

Time heard me as he pass'd,
And his deep, quiet eye
Abash'd me when he spoke,
Moving gravely by:

" For culture, not waste,
Each life is born;
But hours pass alike
Over sands and corn."

But I replied:
Why is good denied?
Thou, Time, art unkind;
The world not to my mind,
And gusty fortune brings vexations
Like sleet on a winter wind.
Then he said with a smile:
" How doth folly beguile!

"Even the little fishes,
    That sport by the river-side,
Must have their wishes
    Sometimes ungratified;
When the ripple above them darkens
    As the sun doth hide,
Great Nature's disregard of them
    May touch their pride;—
Why must a little fish
    Of sunbeams be denied?"

But said I: Life passes
    As we ask, How spend it?
And, before we can determine,
    We perhaps must end it.

But Time replied, compassionate,
    As he is old and grey:
"A minute may be the entrance Gate
    Of a Path to wisdom's Way."

And I said:
    I repent
Of folly and discontent;
    I will turn to-day.
Then deep and soft as Sabbath chime,
Fell on my ears these words of Time:

"Change is hopefully begun
When something is in heart-truth done.
Musing only, all is dark;
Act, and you will strike a spark;

From the spark a taper light ;
Soon a lamp is burning bright.
In every spark is power of fire ;
Another strike, if one expire.

" In love the Maker made each man—
In love for all devised His plan ;
But the wisdom of His love
Is the creature's thought above.
Though thy heart, the reasons shown
Which have satisfied his own,
Darkest methods of that love
Would adoringly approve.

" Oft Event thou wilt not tell,
When Duty yet thou knowest well ;
Finding oft thy will, though free,
Like striving ship upon the sea.
But the wind of stormiest hour
Is a wisdom-guided power ;
And for that in heart-truth done,
God doth care—not thou alone.

A stedfast star, serene and high,
A torch that flares unsteadily,
Are the human will, the will Divine—
A thought of God's, a thought of thine :
As a cloud that dims the day,
Evil for a while hath sway ;
But the bright, undarkening sun
Ever hath the victory won.

" Labours will thy spirit bless
With daily bread of cheerfulness;
Failures will reveal to thee
God's powers of recovery—
From dark necessity shall rise
The life-tree of thy Paradise ;
For the black, uncomely root
Hath power of beauty and of fruit.

" Endure, believing on the Son—
He the Father's heart hath shown;
Then, as swallow in the dark,
Still thou journeyest to a mark ;
Light alone may prove the key,
When darkness makes the mystery.
Living is a mingled dream ;
Dying is the morning beam.

" Since of present things the love
Hath been given thee from above,
The sensuous let thy spirit have
As a body, not a grave ;
Worldly thoughts and joys should be
As rivers running to the sea—
Not as rivulets lost in sand,
Which begin and end on land."

CHAPTER V.

" Upon the top of the pillars was lily-work."—
How mighty and massive is nature's frame!
strong are the world's pillars! yet, what profu-
sion of things graceful, even sportively graceful,
does the earth contain!—beautiful is " the lily-
work!" This great temple, the world, is like
that old temple, the wonder of Solomon's heart
and time—upon the top of the pillars is lily-
work. Sometimes let the heart rejoice in the
establishing strength of the Divine wisdom—
sometimes let it make itself glad with the lily-
work. Pleasantries, lighter acts and utterances,
are to the wise like flowers on the margin of
deep, barge-laden streams—the waters that bear
up and along the works of life, nourish this
flowerage. Man is in the likeness of his Maker
in this also, that small things as well as the great
may have to him dearness, and yield him a good
after their kind. One half-hour, solemnity may

fill his heart; the next, pleasantry; by each
shall his heart be for the time sufficed.

> Solemnly the stars of light
>   In ancient silence show;
> And solemnly the sounding waves
>   Utter their voice below;
> And solemnly the striving winds
>   About the mountains blow;
> And solemnly the beams of dawn
>   Across the countries flow.

In these solemnities is joy. Yet pleasant are
laughter and the dance; and the babble of the
tongue may be health and purity, like that of a
brook. We must let our heart sometimes be a
child—let it entertain itself with wanderings,
gambol, and song.

> The young they laugh: Laughs not the sky?
> The winds they laugh as they pass by;
> The sun he laughs; and nature's face
> Beams with a joyous, laughing grace.
> Yes, laughing; ever she renews
> Her verdant fields, her morning dews;
> Is ever young—the same to-day
> As ages past; and when away
> From earth to heaven we are gone,
> Our dust beneath the turf or stone,
> The moon will smile, the dews distil,
> Dance to the winds the flowers will;
> And round our grave the kindly spring
> Will the cheerful daisies bring.

Have we considered Him who considered the lilies? Have we considered the grand Gospel— that upon the top of its pillars is lily-work? Christ is God come to the household—to settle for us deep things very gravely, but to sympathize with all our naturalness very kindly. Christ is Wisdom; and Wisdom is not harsh-voiced and frowning, but benignant and approachable. It crowns not the slave Toil, suppressing by his stern rule mirth and decoration; but says to man, "If I am thine, then thine also is the earth and the fulness thereof." The world is to the soul a body of death; sins are the grave-clothes. The voice from heaven says, "Loose him, and let him go free." Then the world becomes a body of life, and the soul dwells with it, powerful and glad. Let this our body, the world, and our other body of flesh and bone, have due honour; for they are of a Divine workmanship—bounteous and skilful. Well ruled, they are each "servant made friend;" but ill ruled, they are each slave made lord—and the true lord then has trial of mockings and scourgings very bitter to bear. We may not safely know, as Christians, humanity freed and widely active, unless we know the sanctity of sorrow, the awfulness of conscience, the tran-

G

siency of things visible. But he who knows the heaven rightly, so as to have "days of heaven upon the earth," may as naturally think of passage from earth to heaven as one who sails seawards down a river thinks of his entrance on the width of the ocean. When we have heard Wisdom's reproof and counsel, and have clasped Wisdom's succouring hand, then the more hearty and varied our naturalness, the completer do we become. We shall have a spiritual life and an ordinary that are related—a Father's house in the midst of His estate. There will be home-sanctity and instruction; there will be fields for labour, lawns for sport, gardens full of bloom for varieties of gratification. Then may we so know earth as to speak of the time when "from earth to heaven we are gone," as a time of removal to a grander estate of our Father's, for higher labours and joys. Shall we speak rather of the world having still youth and strength,

> "when away
> We from *earthly love* have gone?"

Whither gone? and how gone? To new love? —or gloomily, as from what we desired should remain? If confidently to new love, then will the first form of the line serve us, nay, be the

better, because hinting in the word "heaven" at
higher love. If sorrowfully, as from love that it
grieves us should cease—strange must we feel
it, that the world laughs on when our voice is
hushed. Why to it is renewing, and to us none?
Shall not the thought of our earthly love ceasing
afflict that love with bitterness, even if there be
no other cause of bitterness? But there is other
cause of bitterness. If we say, "Nature is good,
nature is glad," we must say of man, "Alas for
satieties, stings, frustrations, disappointment!"
Our love of earth, though a real, is yet not a
satisfied love; and so we cannot pass as from
joyous love into forgetfulness, but as from
moving waves of joy and sorrow—on whose
bright crests or in whose shadowed hollows we
changefully are borne—to a land of desire, or to
oblivion beneath the waters. We will sing, and
we will laugh, and will rejoice in the lily-work;
but we will also be "wise of heart" concerning
the "pillars" of the world—the great truths of
conscience, the peril and the worth of free
beings, the saving and perfecting love; by
which truths alone can our well-being and the
well-being of our race be secured. If we have
lived finding our good wholly in things perishable,—then the word of truth is as the inscribing

over the entrance of our palace of delights, the death's-head and the bones, as the symbol of inherent corruptibleness and an appointed perishing; but if we have lived finding the world disappointing and changeful, powerless for a good permanent and pure,—then the word of truth is as the inscribing over our house of mourning, wherein lie the cold remains of departed joy, *Resurgam*—I shall rise again. To some, seriousness is gloom, for it is the showing of death in life; and to others, gloom itself becomes solemnity and sublimity, for to them Wisdom has revealed life in death.

WISDOM.

A mellow wisdom is an autumn sky,
   The blue of which is very pure and pale,
While oft the clouds, rainful and golden rich,
   Follow the course of the leaf-strewing gale,
Or of shadowy moon-white, builded loftily
   Like ships, away into the dimness sail.

For wisdom hath a pure, unsensual love;
   Calm sees the wreck of fading loveliness.
From heart-illumined thoughts its sweetness melts,
   For future strength and fairness earth to bless;
While thoughts, dream-beautiful and stately, move
   New joy in sky-havens distant to possess.

In a valley under a dark rock, a stream by
long beating had formed a hollow, in which its
waters settled, deep and still.   Down from the
brow of the rock hung light and green climbing
plants, dipping themselves into the nourishing
water.   So may there be for a human spirit a
fixed trouble, which overhangs it like a rock,
casting a dark shadow, and keeping off much
sun-light.   Yet the confined, energetic forces of
the soul may slowly make ready a place of
repose.   What is delicate and sportful may
cover the grim face of the stone, and fancies
nourish themselves by the deepest waters of
meditation.   True inward conflict slowly, but
surely, prepares for rest of faith ; then joys, like
plants with foliage of a lighter or a deeper
colouring, will appear, and variously clothe and
adorn.

The little poem that we next give, Theophilus
called " Girl's Evening Wish and Song."   It
was suggested to him by some words of his
mother's. Of her he thus writes :—" My mother,
patient and cheerful in sickness, would watch
with great delight, from her chamber window or
her bed, the evening clouds.   ' Theophilus,' she
would say, ' I should like to be there; I should

like to rest upon them.'   My mother was intense, pious, and simple. She was very sincere
and happy-hearted—rich in sorrows, yet full
of mercy and industry—of a most womanly un-
selfishness. She laughed perfectly. Often,
when we laughed together, I felt like a little
child whom his elder sister catches up, and
dances away with round and round—glad in
myself, yet passive to a higher power of gladness than my own. What my mother did came
like water from a fountain, which says, ' There
is abundance, and there always will be.' Brimful of life, she abounded in useful thoughts, as
a hive does in bees—was of an anger hasty but
healthy, and of a pity very tender and most
practical. Where she came, there came healing
and hope. In love for infants she was a woman
among women. 'Theophilus,' she said, ' you
cannot know, you can never know, the love they
bring with them into the world—it is wonderful!' Her eyes were clear as dew, or fires
on a winter day; yet when I knelt before her
half embracingly, and looked in her face—may
I say it?—half worshippingly, they were to me
as cathedral-aisles, with an altar dimly seen at
the end of the vistas."

GIRL'S EVENING WISH AND SONG.

I would that I might sit
  On that white cloud yonder;
The sunset light around me,
  And the darkening earth under;

A star quite near me,
  The tree-tops far away:
I would kindly look on all the world,
  And for all would pray.

For my heart would larger grow,
  Like the sun in setting;
And my love—its light—would softer be
  Every moment getting.

I would wait till the moon-rise
  Should new beauty bring,
And then in the lonely air
  Thus aloud would sing:—

Oh! the moon in the sky,
With her deep, quiet eye,
She gazes fixedly,
          Down, down.

For Noah in his ark
She lighted the dark,
And did quietly mark
          The world drown.

On the pale-faced dead
Was her pale light shed,
As around they floated
      On the muddy water.

All the trouble that has been
Has the pale moon seen;
And well may we ween
      It has pity taught her.

While the world sleeps under,
And the old seas thunder,
Full of love and wonder
      Is her serious face.

And whether her beams come
To a night-mantled home,
Or a ship amid the foam,
They fall, like a blessing, in every place.

Moon! when our heart is as the sun,
  Fair, like to thee, our thought we find;
Thou shinest seeing the hidden one—
  His mellow'd beam thy lustre kind,
And what is contemplation calm?
  Is it not heart-light from the mind?

Theophilus appends a note to this. "Are not," writes he, "these last lines a little un-girlish? Perhaps so; and yet womankind well knows, what mankind ought never to forget, that there cannot be bright, tranquil thoughts without glowing affections. *Moon*shine is sun-shine softened."

———•———

Heard to-night, at sun-set, the plash of a brook—saw the shooting of the ice fibres on a still water—watched the mists gather on the horizon—looked the sun in the face as he retired —listened to the browse of the sheep as they cropped the grass—saw them go on the knee, the better to take their food; then beheld the tranquillizing moon-rise. What a great silence, and yet what a great activity there was! I had a quiet, solemn sense of the living God. He is also the loving God. On a wintry day, what strange loveliness often comes towards evening! The fading light, like a fading forest, shows wonderful colours. The wind has broken and discomfited the dark ranks of clouds. The zenith glows like the ceiling of a cheerful, fire-lighted room. Star-graced bits of blue appear,

of different shades, like flowers newly opened.
Fresh stars beam on us momently, with a look
of surprise, as of persons who, waking suddenly,
find the night gone and morning glowing. Perhaps there is the moon, and near it greenish
tints, finely contrasting with its own soft white.

> Many hours wet and dull
> Bring on an hour beautiful.
> This winter day in darkness rose,
> Yet hath it beauty at its close.
> Fairest colours now we see,
> Because the rains fell heavily.
> And thus it is that present gloom
> Prepares a beauty that shall come—
> Beauty which, in one bright hour,
> Of long dark countervails the power.
> Soon stirrings of delight begin,
> And back its peace the heart doth win.
> Thus, too, a life's rain-troubled day
> May glorious grow in its decay;
> Familiar earth, now partly hidden,
> Partly reveal'd the higher heaven—
> Of sorrow and of care the traces
> An evening loveliness effaces;
> And as the full-starr'd darkness nears,
> The twilight calmest beauty wears.
> Soft grows the heart, because it sadden'd,
> And with a hope in joy is gladden'd;
> For hope within a joy hath place,
> As star within a skyey place;

And hope as star, to heart as eye,
Beams from a far reality.
Now, gradual, earth withdraws from view,
As fades a bloom each evening hue
Dims, but to reveal on high
A lofty templed majesty.
In love, and with a calm delight,
We meet the still and solemn night.

It was at another season of the year that
Theophilus, sitting by a river side, made the
poem that follows :—

EVENING.

Trees grow dark against the sky,
Darkly runs the river by,
Mists upon the meadows lie.

Half seen the cattle browse or rest,
The lark has fallen to his nest,
Cloudy curtains fold the west.

Above, along the unfurrow'd deep,
Racks of clouds slowly sweep,
New-born stars begin to peep.

The fragrant haystack, high and wide,
Finish'd is—the men with pride
Descend the ladder by the side.

The pony views with eye askance
The man with stealthy steps advance,
Fearing lest he begin to prance.

The bird now houses in the thatch,
Many a hand is on the latch,
And dogs begin their nightly watch.

Gnats unseen near us hum,
Bats like timid spectres come,
Black-bodied beetles boom.

Fish within their margin pool,
Of flowing river-water full,
Floating rest, asleep and cool.

A shutting gate, voices clear,
Then a heavy tread we hear,
Then a light foot passing near.

Now day is dead, and dews weep,
Sable shadows round us creep;
And the night is queen, her empire sleep.

MEDITATIVE HINTS CONCERNING PLEASURE AND SADNESS.

If we do not heed the claim of the different appetites of our nature, we exasperate them, and they attain the fever strength of starvation.

The pampered and the starved each cry out for food; but we must distinguish carefully between their cryings. The starved heart may hunger for a meal of approbation, of joy, of love. A supply of well-flavoured pleasure will moderate rather than exasperate a sensuous craving. Kindly appreciative words may bring upon the spirit of a man a softening dew of humility, instead of feeding within him the boisterous flame of vanity. That the soul be without pleasure is not good, any more than that it be without knowledge. We may say, Take a little pleasure for thine heart's sake, and thine often infirmities. There are those who desire happiness, as the intemperate desire wine; yet will we not forget that the wines of cheerfullizing pleasure are serviceable.

Those good angels, who can be and are both "lovers of pleasures" and "lovers of God," because they desire not five cups when three suffice, and sleep not lulled by the brook's murmuring, when drinking of it they should lift up the head refreshed, and go forward to fight against evils; these good angels, if they know and notice our way on earth, must see much to amuse and offend them. There are some of us who seem to think that we compliment God's heaven by

despising His earth, and show our sense of the
great things the future man may do yonder, by
counting as utterly worthless all that the present
man may do here. There is joy upon the earth,
which, though earthly, is not impure—which,
though vanishing, is real. Shall we be the
brighter spirits for being the duller men? Is the
breath that cries, "Vanity, Vanity!" the most
acceptable incense that can rise to heaven?
Dissatisfied, querulous, sombre-minded persons,
who have no eye for the graceful decorations or
gorgeous splendours of the world—who live,
speak, and act, as if all were woeful, and the
supreme duty of man ever to cry, "Woe is me!"
—these are shunned and hated. It is believed
that this their dull sadness, caricaturing solemnity, is affected and heartless; but if not, that
it is disease—piteous, yet loathsome. He who
shrouds his soul in haircloth, and clouds his face
with gloom—who acts as if truth were the slave-
owner, and duty the whip—must surely seem
very ridiculous in the eyes of the angels. But
what of the man who lives as if life were a joke,
as if all solemnity of thought, all deep feeling,
all anxious fear, were disease? Such a man as
this the angels must scorn. He is of the evil
one; and towards the dark places, where the evil

one scourges the foolish, do his steps advance.
But to these two classes—the light men and the
dull men—there are doubtless persons seeming
to belong respectively, at whom the angels laugh
kindly, and over whom they lament charitably.
Dulness may mean well, and lightness not mean
ill; yet are they, nevertheless, dulness and lightness—not solemnity, not happiness. How the
world still calls out for happiness, as after a
thing not attained and yet attainable! Its
moon still waxes and wanes, as the foolish world
still stretches out its arms for it; yet it shines in
our face with pleasant beams, though itself may
never be clasped and embraced. Much discus-
sion has there been about happiness—much will
there be. Philosophies die or transmigrate; but
the happiness question comes up in all new ones,
or all new forms of old ones. It is like the daily-
bread question—one for all generations. And
it were well if it were treated as a daily-bread
question; but it is made a daily-cake question.
Now, daily cake is not attainable; and if it
were attainable, would not be wholesome. The
hungry soul cannot always get the honeycomb;
so it seeks a loaf; and then, when it can get
honey also, finds it the sweeter. The full soul
loathes even the honeycomb, yet cries, " Give,

give! but something sweeter than the honey-comb!—not that!" Now, there is nothing sweeter. What then is to be done? The fault is in the appetite, not in the honey. And that can only renew itself by allowing activity to other needy parts of the nature—can only find its honey remaining sweet, or even perhaps becoming sweeter, as itself is co-ordinated with what else there is in man. Often when we *want*, it is not we truly, but a part of us, that wants; this our appetite soon finds its "chief good" as alone, attainable. Then it has grief: nothing more remains to "conquer;" and the honey "conquered," gotten, has become vanity. The whole loves its parts; but then the parts must love and honour the whole. Good loves pleasures; but then pleasures must love and honour good. The angels relish their angel-cake abidingly, perhaps increasingly; but then they do not put cake for bread, nor make the eating of cake ever new, their " chief good."

In the happiness questioning, men have debated the "chief good." What woe for us had any of the thousand decisions been discoveries! —if we had been able to say, " This is our best thing; it may be had, and it is all that may be had!" Men debating the chief good are like termites debating the highest height—meaning their own highest hill; a structure really high and wonderful for them. But then there are human structures that they know not of—and so are there Divine structures, alps and worlds. He who, in his darkened study, with closed eyes, and diligent, thinking heart, shall think out for us a true plan of "the Jerusalem which is above," is the man who may find for us the "chief good." And who shall this man be but that villager, who, by "original thought," has mapped out London and described it, with its streets and squares—all its wonderfulness and all its sin? Let search be made for this man, and, when discovered, let him have utmost honour and estimation. Pleasures are so often not good, that when we say, Good is pleasant, or brings pleasantness—which is always true—we seem to speak falsely, because we use inadequate words. Pleasure that satisfies and rejoices the appetite for a while may change its nature, and prove, too, that in former pleasing it has hurt the man. So, to say that good gives *pleasure*, seems poor expression of the truth that it blesses us. Good shall satisfy and rejoice the man, as what man has called pleasure does the appetite; but with a higher rejoicing—a new pleasure so above

H

the old, that he likes not even to name it pleasure.

Pleasures to the animals are good, because they are joys in order and degree according to their being; and they put out their strength duly for them, and are not mere passive receivers. Our pleasures are good when, in order and degree, they are according to our being— when we are not passive indulgers merely, but active, as with Him who worketh all in all. Now, in this world, man not only developes, grows, but developes as a free being in the midst of good and evil. Often he takes not up in his thought of the good, the Right, that which is, according to the order of the Supreme Wisdom, demandable of him when known, and according to which, as unknown, he must be treated. We are training not alone to have, but to do—to have and to do according to God's having and doing; training for self-activity in loving community, according to laws that relate to a gradually unfolding and eternal life. So the world is very complex; partly we have knowledge, partly not. We are to be partakers of the Divine knowing, in order that we may perfectly have and do. But greatly are we agitated with questions which, unless we act

according to what we know as demandable, and
"lay hold" of the Divine assuring words, " I
am," and "I am love," will hopelessly agitate us.
Because of life beyond life, in the spiritual
world, the tangles of good and evil, else enigmas
hopeless and torturing, become hieroglyphics
full of profound and hopeful significance.   The
earth, with its miseries and wickedness, is like a
huge bemired root ; out of which, foul and dark
as it is, strength, beauty, and majesty shall
spring.   But they who hope thoughtfully, hope
seriously; and knowing sin, that it is, and
works, and must be destroyed, deal veraciously
with the facts of life—with man's sadness and
joy.   The wise, affirming that the universe
exists for the fullest manifestation of the love
of God to created being—that the earth has
beauty, and existence gladness—yet remember
that God the Judge is real, death real, future
destiny real, a hunger for redemption real, and
a redeeming Christ real.   The words and the
ways of these wise may seem to many to
betoken the cold, gloomy, unjoyous heart ; yet
is theirs truly the heart that, befriending gaiety,
can console sorrow.   They look not despond-
ingly upon the world ; yet will they have a
knowledge of the worst, as of the best.

They regard the antics and foolery of the worldly gay as very like the pranks of madmen; yet rather win to soberness by the exhibition of a cheerfulness—which, because serious, is sted-fast—than seek to control, but at the same time provoke, by an imposed strait-waistcoat of sanctimony. These separate not the Divinely-ordained helpers. They set not the earth against the heaven, gaiety against wisdom, business against poetry, devoutness against the worldly life, wit against sense, tears against laughter. Seeing that the world hates taking thought of sins, and bears readily with exaggeration of the mirthful, because of its griefs, but dislikes those much affected with the gravely impressive views of life, because in them is reproof; the wise, the wiser they grow, become the more careful to live and to speak with love in all their truth. Men often are they of a sad heart, yet of a hopeful word and endeavour.

When seriousness and sadness are generous and manly, we shall ever find that they have far more sympathy and allowance for the gay, than either the innocent or the foolish gay have or can have for them. A man whom wisdom makes sad, strives forward to the seeing and possessing of a just happiness. The world, and himself with the world, he hopes and believes will find that the good and the right are one, and wisdom one with them; the good ordaining the right by wisdom; the right, also, leading on to the good by wisdom. There will be freer scope for the light-heartedness of many in heavenly worlds than ever they have had on earth. Yet in the daily life of those who have seemed in solemn massiveness of character like frowning rocks, there have been, seen only by God and the few who loved them, graces, gentleness, and hilarity, abundant and beautiful; even as among the dark rocks are sheltered recesses, in which are found delicate ferns, and flowers of beautiful growth and rare fragrance. Every good thing, and every pleasant thing of the earth, should be acknowledged, rejoiced in, and truly befriended by Christians. That which is of the earth, earthly, is wonderfully connected with and dependent upon what is of the heaven, heavenly; as the round, fruitful world is dependent upon and connected with the encircling air. We must have an inward life of heavenly thought, and purpose, and hope, in order guiltlessly and relishingly to partake of diversified natural joys. We must heed and lawfully satisfy our various appetites for such joys, if we are not to feel that the truths concerning sin and discipline, Divine rule and the future, have only a power of gloom and cursing.

The spirit of our Christianity is domesticity and humanity, working in us a sadness by which the heart is made better; and then joyfulness, with a pure conscience. In a sunny place where are orchards, and groves, and gardens, who would make all desolate, under pretence of letting the sun be seen? The trees may need thinning, the gardens weeding, that they may be the more healthy and beautiful, and that the sun may have more effect upon their life and beauty—for our good and their own they need this. But the sun is honoured in their perfection and their serviceableness. So is the spiritual honoured in the secular; so is the supreme Sun, God, honoured, as the "things of man" more and more perfectly minister to the well-being of man.

We will close this chapter with a poem, in which Theophilus gives expression to changing moods of exultation, fear, religious adoration, and Christian peace.

MODULATIONS.

My God, I love the world,
  I love it well—
Its wonder, and fairness, and delight—
  More than my tongue can tell;
And ever in my heart, like morning clouds,
  New earth-loves rise and swell.

Lilies I love, and stars,
  Dewdrops, and the great sea;
Colour, and form, and sound,
  Combining variously;
The rush of the wind, and the overhanging vast—
  Voiceless immensity.

Thou world-creator art,
  World-lover too;
In delight didst found the deep,
  In delight uprear the blue;
And with an infinite love and carefulness
  The wide earth furnish through.

My God, I am afraid of Thee, I am afraid—
  Thou art so silent, and so terrible;
And oft I muse upon Thee in the deep night dead,
  Listening as for a voice that shall my spirit tell,
  To be of comfort and of courage, for that all is well.

Of thoughts uncounted as the stars,
Which burn undimm'd from old eternity,
Oh, everlasting God !
    Thy Spirit is a sky—
A brighten'd dark, enrounding every world
    With stillness of serenest majesty :
Fit several forms of the same splendour
Thou to beholding worlds dost render,
In starry wonder of a thousand skies,
Beheld by creature-eyes :
Who in the glorious part have symbol bright
Of the uncomprehended Infinite.

But if as the great dark art Thou, unknown,
    Thou, God reveal'd, art as the sweet noon blue ;
Soft canopying mercy in the Christ is shown,
    And the azure of His jove Thy face beams through,
Looking forth, like the sun, to comfort and to bless,
And with beauty over-lighting the rough wilderness.

CHAPTER VI.

WHEN—

The butterfly hides, the snail homes in his shell,
And closed is the eye of the bright pimpernel,

there is, said Theophilus, other hiding, and
homing, and closing of the eyes. That dear
little mollusk, infant man, is hidden : it is not
sunny enough by the hedge-rows for his appearance; infancy is now homed in its sacred
tabernacle — the cradle, likely enough with
closed eyes. They will open soon; for infancy is wakeful as the lark, though its early
song is not always so pleasing as the bird's.
But shall we ungenerously define an infant
to be—a thing that sucks and screams? Truly
it does both, but how much more is it, and
does it! Diamonds taken from light shine
awhile in the dark; so eyes of infants, fresh
from heaven, have for a while on the earth

strange heavenliness.   The wonderful little face,
how simple, yet how venerable it is! the little
being, how necessitous, and yet how trusting!
Well housed and well provided, without thought
of rent and taxes; milk, and honey, and water-
springs, all about it.

> Oft on sunny days espying,
>   On the nurse or mother's arm,
> A draperied babe serenely lying
>   Bosom-shelter'd, warm;
> Half in smiles, and half in sighing,
>   I bless the babe from harm.
>
> This dimpled, innocent beginner,
>   Who hath yet no evil done,
> And of tenderest smiles the winner,
>   Hath no sorrow known;
> Like the rest will prove a sinner,
>   Boy or maiden grown.

Yet. neither the soiled lily nor the stricken
bird receive their hurt because of the forgetfulness of Him who is over all.   Mouldable,
merry, undoubting infancy will grow into a
being, unshapely, confused, and sad; but so
good a beginning is hopeful prophecy of a good
ending.   An innocent no man may die; but
we have the "sentence of death" written on

our good and happiness—why? That they should perish? No; but that we should not trust in them, but in the "Living One," from whom they and their life are. Infancy is scattered over the earth as vital seed, not to be quickened except it die; but appointed to die, that it may fully live. We will honour the mother, and will rejoice in the children. And whilst the mother shall specially know the wonder, and beauty, and sorrow, and hope of maternity, we will yet join with her in her honour the many unmarried and childless, but truly motherly, women, by whom, as under soft wings, the weak, the sick, the uninstructed, and the young, are sheltered and comforted. The childless may be most motherly; and as those who "watched the stuff" shared with those who fought the battle, so at least should they share in the mother's honours.

But who would see a fair sight? Let him, when the mother is shining as the sun in her household, look upon her and her fair planetary company. She, at least, looks as if she had found the work of her life, and were doing it with all her heart. And though evil families abound, shall caricature and roving beggary make us forget beauty and the peace of homes?

We bury the dead out of our sight; and we must not let those who, in any sense, are dead while they live, spoil with their loathliness our joy at the sight and presence of the living.

Here, again, is another vision of the mother " in her beauty :"—

THE MOTHER.

A babe doth rest upon her breast,
   It is her latest bloom;
A hidden bud she cherisheth,
   That soon to light will come.

And lovely is the open flower,
   Freshly sweet and fair;
And wondrous is the forming bud,
   Warm-shrouded from the air.

Dear as to Eve the stainless blooms
   Of Eden's central tree,
Are, Mother! to thy heart the babes
   That blossom forth from thee.

The clustering valley-lilies white
   Have soft broad leaves above;
And safely grow the innocents,
   Shielded by mother's love.

The presence of childhood in the world, and the contemplation of it—how great power have

these in healing wounds of the heart and dis-
persing melancholies! The balm of the nursery
is as the "balm of Gilead." The physician
there works wonders. Though the mother is in
watchings oft, in weariness and painfulness, she
has her "joy hidden in sorrow." And who is
there that, seeing the merry, secure, free, innocent, unburdened child, does not feel that as the
child is so he would be? The child seems so
full of life, like a river brim full—as if always
like morning, and always sunny. This unex-
hausting vigour of life—the fresh interest the
world inspires—the eagerness about all things—
these the man feels have left himself. But
even infancy has its sharp, small troubles. Its
mornings are not without clouds. Soon enough
self-will and waywardness show themselves;
and early the question will become with the
child, as with the man—rather, Who shall be
greatest? than, Who shall be best? And yet
not falsely we speak of happy childhood. Who
ever heard of a self-sufficient babe? And, for a
while "separate from sinners," these young ones
are "harmless and undefiled." So childhood
may fitly speak to man words of good and hope,
and may externally represent to him a likeness
to the budding of his inward Best. When he

feels within him stirrings of the better, these are as a budding childliness—an activity of his truest self—himself becoming as a little child. We are to be ever putting away childish things, and yet ever renewing the childly temper—the temper of loving trust, simple docility.   And since, when we have attained, we are still called to attain ; as growing well-doers, we may possess a perpetual childliness that does not exclude manhood.   Comparing the man of full age with the little one yet a babe, the man is the more developed, but the babe the more perfect in its own stage of being.   So our childliness of heart will show us more of what is best in us than the imperfect speech and deed of that which in us has attained manhood.   Childliness and man-hood may be, in "spirits made perfect," not alone equally real, but equally good.   But with us childliness is the better.   Our growths pre-sent themselves as blemished and irregular. Childliness, which is to be ever the beginning of new experiences and labours, is by its betterness a source of purifying spirit and wisdom for growths already of some age.   So we are to become and to remain childly, that we may be the better men : then our labours and difficul-ties, as men, will bring us renewings of simple-

heartedness; and thus childliness and manliness
will be mutually helpful. " Of such is the
kingdom of heaven." But if any make themselves childish rather than childly, thinking to
become children in faith by becoming such in
knowledge—these are of the dark kingdom of
ignorance. When faith in the man has become
childly, it is yet a higher thing than the faith of
the child. The child trusts the mother whose
breasts nourish it. The man gets not his sustenance easily, as milk from the breast; but by
labours, as bread from the ground. Trust, for
his bread and all his good, may come only after
harassing doubts. When it shows itself, then,
as truly childly, it is a higher faith than the
child's. The child's mind works early and
much; but it does not work to find out the
principles on which it should work. Long
before the child cares, or is able to ask the
question, What is Truth? it knows much; and
has a happy certainty, which the man may well
desire for himself. The child's uncareful certainty is, as certainty, more perfect than the
man's; yet is the man's certainty attained after
doubt and debating, the higher; and the more
childly it becomes, the less childish is it. Manly
inquiries are high and honest exercisings of the

conscience and heart: painful and toilsome they may be, but the issue is a happy, childlike sureness. The childish, who inquire not, rebuke the doubt and debate of sincere inquirers, urging them to become as babes; yet themselves may be far less babes than the men they rebuke. Arrogant for ignorance such often show themselves, with a most unchildly scorn; while they who say earnestly, What, what is Truth? may already be the more childly for their questioning, and are on the way to childly faith and sureness. The young man's doubt may be but the child's faith dying to grow.

With a prose extract from one of Theophilus's books, we will introduce a ballad of his—a favourite with him. This ballad is a lowly domestic blossom, looking brightly in at the parlour-window, when the rain and wind have hurt rarer and loftier plants. Over the prose extract is written—

"MANY SUCH THINGS ARE WITH HIM."

It was winter, and there were heavy rains and much sickness. Andrian, fatigued and suffering from a cold, was invited to attend the funeral of one of his deceased patients. From regard to her and her friends, he imprudently went; but, used to exposures, he went without much fear. The day was wet and cold; and as he stood by the grave, he felt he was wounded, but knew not that it was fatally. Death was with him when he returned from the dead. For some days he was ill, and as much as possible he rested; but one evening, returning early for a few additional hours of sleep, soon after he had lain down he heard his surgery-bell ring violently. He rang his own, that he might know what was wanted. The messenger was from one seized with sudden and dangerous sickness. On learning this, Andrian rose at once, and ordered his horse. "Surely," said his wife, "you will not go, ill as you are?" "Mary," said he, "something must be instantly done, or the man will die." Very sorrowfully she closed the door, as the sound of his horse's gallop died away. All night he was absent, and at day-break he returned weary and very ill. Retiring to his bed, he remained there through the day. That day, Mary did for him all that the disciplined ingenuity of love could devise. The next morning, as she was preparing his breakfast in the parlour, his bell rang. She was by his side before it had ceased sounding; but when she

I

entered, he lay as the dead, smitten senseless. If moments may be discriminated, the first was of agony, the second of prayer, the third of wise action. Instantly she despatched messengers to a surgeon and physician, both attached friends of Andrian's. Though they were each able to arrive shortly, they arrived in vain. "Culverson," said the surgeon earnestly, "we must save him; we must!" The physician shook his head. What could be done was done; but that night a new name was entered on God's book of widows.

The history of widows—what a marvellous chapter of sorrow and mercy it would form in a history of man! If the wind be tempered for shorn lambs, yet it blows upon them; if for the sick God make all their bed in their sickness, yet it is to a bed, and that of languishing, they are confined; and so if the widow and the fatherless are God's charge, it is as those appointed to a harassed, striving life that they receive help and comfort.

THE SAILOR AND HIS MOTHER.

A widow mother had a lad,
  Now sixteen years was he;
And nothing would content his heart,
  But he must go to sea.
Then said the widow, " God is great
  Upon both sea and land;
And sailor people he must have,
  And lives are in his hand."

So, with many thoughts of waves and rocks,
She put a Bible in his box;
  And as he took the key,
She gave him in her tears a kiss,
Saying, " William, when you read in this,
  You'll often think of me."

To comfort her at home was left
  Two daughters and a son :
She loved them much, but often thought
  About her sailor one.
Sometimes she said, " He's surely lost,"
When soon a letter came by post,
  With William's writing on;
And as they all the letter read,
The widow raised her eyes and said,
" How very thankful we should be
To hear good news from one at sea !"

Sometimes, with hope that all was well,
There came a curious bird or shell
　　From some far place at sea;
Sometimes a letter money bore—
He sent it, wishing it was more,
　　To help the family;
And then around the times would come
When he left his ship to visit home,
　　With his mother dear to be:
And when she saw him tall and strong,
The widow thought no more how long
　　She had waited patiently;
But she said, "How quickly time has flown!
And William, boy, how much you've grown
　　Since first you went to sea!"

Now his brother James, the carpenter,
　　Was rising by degrees,
And both the sisters married were,
　　With little families—
When home came William with a wife;
　　Born far away was she;
Her accent foreign, dark her face;
She had a woman's truth and grace,
　　And loved him tenderly.
And he kiss'd her, and call'd her "Dearest life!"
　　And said, "Mother, she has shared with me
　　In many perils of the sea."

The pitying mother hears a tale
　　Of dangers on the sea;
How dark the night, how strong the gale,
　　How nearly drown'd was he:

And then she says, " God bless thee, lad !
It makes my old heart very glad
　　Your face once more to see."

The widow now was growing grey—
　　Warm-hearted still was she ;
And William's wife she often told
　　How good a son was he.
And then she said, " This weary head
　　Soon in its rest will be."

And sickness came, and death drew near ;
And once, when all around her were,
As William from the Scripture read,
She on the pillow raised her head,
　　Saying, " William, give it to me."
Then in her trembling hand she took
An old and well-worn little book ;
And said, with a tear, " Why, William, this
Is the Bible I gave you with my kiss
　　When first you went to sea."

Soon William stood by his mother's grave,
His tears as salt as any wave,
　　His breast heaved like the sea ;
And the years of voyage he had known,
Came all at once, not one by one,
　　Back to his memory.

Then sadly home to his wife he went,
And, with head upon her bosom bent,
He said, " Oh, never was a man—
No, never since the world began—

With a better mother blest ! "
And she answer'd, with her tenderest kiss,
" It is true, it is true, I know it is ;
But William, dearest, think of this—
    She's quietly at rest.'

From another note-book we extract the following; it relates to the Necessities of the Orphan and the Weak :—

An imagined absurdity may sometimes best illustrate a real wrongness. We will suppose the improbable, to show the folly and sin of what is quite real and quite frequent in actual life. It is a winter day, and a father stands at his parlour-window with his infant on his arm. Snow is on the ground. Near the window is a thorn-tree, with its ripe, red berries. Birds alight on the tree, scatter the snow, and eat the berries. It was in part for the birds that the berries have ripened.

The father looks up and says—" How kind is God ! This is His providence ; He feeds the birds." And he speaks wisely and piously. But now, ringing the bell—" Nurse," he says, " see how God is feeding the birds ! take our baby, and set him in the snow; God will care for him." So baby is set in the snow; and the rough wind soon extinguishes the tender flame of his life. Then the father cries—"What a dark providence! how inscrutable are the ways of God!" Are there not many like this supposed strange father, who talk of providence but as an excuse for their leaving those whom they were expressly appointed to cherish and help, to stumble on unwatched, and front as they may—with souls, and perhaps bodies, unclad and unhoused—the "bitter blast" of time? There are not wanting, too, men who, opening the window of their comfortable room, call out to the miserable to trust in God; and then, exhausted by the effort and chilled with the entering wind, turn round to the fire, and refresh themselves with wine, cake, and essays on philanthropy. It will often be, that our best help to men is by our reminding them of higher help than ours. But how do we remind them? By a human kindness that represents and testifies of the Divine. Often men cannot feel and believe they have a father, till they find they have brothers. Believing in man, they can believe in God. While life is wintry and desolate, the help of a true-voiced, true-handed person bears witness of the Divine goodness. Thanks

for the help merges in thanks to the man;
thanks to the man, in a glow of heart towards
" the Father in heaven."　Then arise spiritual
hopes and remembrances, like first flowers while
the season is yet dead; whose fragrance seems
both to bring back the spring season of other
years, and to make the coming spring present.
Sometimes, when the experiences of life have
made the issues of thought from the heart unhealthy, the spirit is barren of growths devout.
and wise; then acts of humanity are like the
salt which the prophet cast into the fountain
of an ancient barren land, which healed the
waters, so that the land blossomed.　When we
speak of care for the weak and the orphan, we
do not mean just a provision for them of sugar
and other pleasant things.　We say, pityingly,
" Alas, for that poor boy! there's nobody to
whip him."　Restraints are necessary, and the
merciful, forecasting man, must in his kindness
sometimes seem unkind.　But we affirm that
men are constituted for one another, Stewards
of Divine Answers.　The world cannot, and
no man can fully, answer the question of his
own life.　For the babe's seeking, the breast of
the mother is a happy finding.　For the world's
seeking, Christ is the Divine Answer—a Hu-

manity witnessing of Goodness, casting heavenly salt into the fountain of worldly thought. For the want of the orphan, for the practical question of his needy life, stewards of mercies and wisdom must be then stewards of answers. It is true, according to the so often quoted fable of the Sphinx, that man has questions put to him, which, if he cannot answer, he is devoured. But it is not true, that it is merely a man's own blame if he cannot answer. A man who may have wisdom is free to neglect it, and then certain to have death or grief, as there comes a lesser or a final questioning which he cannot answer. But show us the man who, out of his own head and courage, has fully answered the question of the Sphinx of Life. There is no such man. The brave and true will find many just answers; but they will surely often hear God saying, by fact or by friend, "I will answer for thee." And if there be helpless ones, for whom no stewards of answers can be found, then they must be devoured. But this is not a final devouring; alive in the "belly" of their sorrow, amidst the great dark waves of change, the jaws of their grave shall unclasp, and they, like Jonah, find again light and the land—the light and the land of this world, or of another.

Theophilus knew what is demanded of a man's self, and knew also the dangers of the "philanthropic "way of viewing the world. Here are two other extracts from his note-book:—

It is ennobling, yet humbling, to feel that we have distinct reality—a will of our own. With how much are we entrusted! yet with what danger and difficulty are we encompassed, moving onward in much ignorance, and amid many enticements! As we consider how much depends on ourselves—how the healthy unfolding of our being rests greatly with us—our high consciousness of manhood would be swallowed up in our fear of failure, could we not look to the All-powerful for strength and guidance. Yet did we hear a voice saying, " Rest quietly; God and thy friend will do all for thee "—our good we should receive with selfish, ungrateful joy— our evil crouch before with fear and hatred. But when we hear a voice saying, "This is the work I have given thee to do," as we think on its greatness, we cry, "Lord, help us!" The weak flesh, the wayward mind, the rough, windy world, cause the continuing well-doer to know the reality of his own will, the supremacy of God's. Such a one discouraged remits effort, then renews it under a kindling sense of obligation, and feels himself in his act—knows that he can, and so feels that he ought. Yet so limited is he, so vainly wishful, and so early his necessity sounds curfew, and he must extinguish the forge-fire of his endeavours, that he says, "How vain, how weak is man! how mighty his Maker!" And yet again, so frequently has he failed after succeeding a little, that he has learned to expect failures, and is sure that new success awaits him. So, weaker because of flesh or circumstance than other men, such a one yet has a might of patience, and a power of renewing endeavour, that the strong and prospering often want. Orphans, and solitaries, and the afflicted, may show us that the weak are the strong, and the lacking the complete. Their mind, hardened to trouble as the blacksmith's hand to fire, like that hand is skilled and serviceable. Grievous is the solitude of compelled isolation; yet he to whom the "city of stirs" and the crowded market are forbidden, may in privacy gain some insight into the wonder of every man's being by an exacter study of his own heart. He cannot travel over the countries, so he watches the heaven and his garden, and becomes learned in clouds and flowers. His greetings, too, and companionship, are rather with the dead that live, than with the living that are dead. But, be a man more or less equally yoked with that nearer world the body, and that other body the world, he can neither obtain his good nor subdue his evil without the union of a real endeavour of his own with a real trust in the Divine aid. If a man says " Yes " to God, then God says " Yes " to him. Divine Truth and Wisdom are ground and sunny air for such man's growing life. The greater his girth and stature, and the deeper his root strikes, the more ground he grasps, the more air and light appropriates. And the evil in man, it is not like the core in the apple, which may be at once cut away; the " carnal mind " is not a tumour that may be removed by a short, sharp appliance of the knife. It is an unhealthiness, which for cure will require seventy times seven dippings in the waters of life, and habitual exercisings on the hills of truth.

We must beware alike of misanthropy, and of philanthropy so called. A thorn is a changed bud. Sad it is for budding kindness to become thorny misanthropy. We wish to be loved and considered; and every body seems faulty,

and cold, and disagreeable; so we hate, or
seem to hate, because we were so loving. Our
budding kindliness has changed into a sharp,
censuring thorn of discontent. But are we not
deceived in thinking we have love enough to
do for the world, what we are surprised to find
the world has not love enough to do for us?
The philanthrope may avow rather sentiments
of which he would have the advantage, than of
which he would give the advantage. And philanthropy is often not the love of man, but the
love of being thought to love him; and how
different the love of any thing, from the love
of being thought to love it! Such philanthropy
is a modern accomplishment; and the heartless
may give us fluent talk about loving sentiments,
as the unmusical may rattle off showy tunes.
And where philanthropy is not such a mere
"accomplishment," it may yet indicate Need
rather than Charity. As a man is a Radical
till his fortunes are rooted, cries "Change" till
he prospers, and then becomes Conservative and
says, "Let well alone:" so he may be well-
disposed till he is well off; philanthropic till
he is comfortable; and then, parting company
with want, he parts with sympathy for the
needy. The man called misanthrope may prove

to be the more philanthropic. If having at all
the "good heart," we must needs love men;
but if in want, must needs so often hunger
vainly for their help, that sorrow and indigna-
tion, because of the world's selfish, unthorough
way, must largely possess us: yet these may
not only consist with truest practical kindness,
but may have given that kindness its purity and
permanence. Nay, must not a true hate and
a true love of much that is human be found
together, if either hate or love is to exist justly
and safely in our heart?

We all suffer from the want of genuine human
help and sympathy. But often, to meet our
particular case, it is required that those around
us possess a higher than the average goodness.
We must not curse humanity because we cannot
find the man we want. They who do not see
or feel for us, may yet see much and feel for
many. Our love, if we really would show kindness as well as receive it, may fitly make that
rule its own, on which our anger so often seems
to act—To do to others as we have *not* been
done by. It is beautiful to see an injured,
disappointed man, protective and kindly. What
then shall we say of the glowing humanity of
the young, who are sure to meet with more or

less injury and disappointment? They are deceived as to the power of their kindly thought and purpose, yet they are not false: goodness, which will not bear a heavy weight or a sudden strain, may yet be real. It is pleasant—how pleasant!—amidst the general leafy vitality of the young heart, to see these blossomings of just, kind sentiment. For if the thorn is a transformed bud, the blossom is a transformed leaf. The leaf of youth's own fresh experience becomes the blossom of a kind and good wish for others. The blossoms will outnumber the fruits; but, at least, the fruits cannot outnumber the blossoms. So then, if, where there is much blossom, there must yet be some disappointment, we well remember that where there is little blossom, there can be but small hope.

There was a pear-tree in his garden, which, Theophilus said, he regarded with gratitude and respect: it was a worthy, encouraging tree. It was very full of blossom usually; the fruits, not numerous, but most excellent—juicy, sweet, and large. How admirable of the tree! said he; so many blooms in vain, and yet to do so well. How encouraging! A man may not realize the tenth part of what he wished and purposed, and yet may be a man not alone bearing fruit, but fruits rarely good.

Of how it is with the vine, and how it may be with the young, here is a cheerful word in the poem with which we will close this chapter.

THE VINE.

Prune ye the vine, and carefully
    Despoil it of its leafy show;
More rich and full the streams of life
    Will to the enlarging clusters flow;
And as the days to autumn darken,
    Into ripeness these will darken too.

But curse not the luxuriance,
    The leafiness of early spring:
In power of leaf is power of life,
    And when to swell the grapes begin,
Each leaf will from the rains and air,
    Material for sweetness win.

Early within the leafy shades,
    The uncolour'd, modest flowers appear;
From far, unscented and unseen,
    Of delicate, sweet fragrance near,
And deck'd for the wise examining eye,
    In organic orderliness fair.

A vine-blossom is an early love,
　An early thought or purpose good :
Mid leafy screens of common hours
　It grows unmark'd in solitude,
Fragrant and fair, though unobserved,
　And of rich fruits the cluster-bud.

And in the years and months of Life,
　That branching vine, with ragged bark,
The ripe expansion of the fruit,
　In utterances and deeds we mark,
As large, and sweet, and numerous,
　As grapes of rounded beauty dark.

The wise, the young heart's leafiness
　Will prune with care, not angrily :
Note indications half-reveal'd
　Of what and where the fruit will be ;
See miniature grapes in cluster-buds,
　From the fragrance learn their quality.

CHAPTER VII.

I TRAVELLED yesterday on a railway, in that indifference of spirit that succeeds the flood and tumult of a great sorrow. I felt a wild sense of security—What matter now if I be dashed dead? I am as dead. I am withered as a sea-plant torn from its rock: let the wind and the tide sport with me as they will. But even that moment, when thus my soul spoke, there arose a thought in which was comfort. As the smell of the sea cleaves to the sea-plant for long years, so the love of the dead clings to the living; so shall my love remain with me. This was the thought. And presently, as I looked across the ever-opening and changing country, saw the tree-girt homes, the cattle, the farms, and the villages, I grew happy, sacredly happy, without wishing it; and, as I wished it not, so neither could I prevent it. I watched not for the morning, yet it came. I could no more hinder the quickening of my life, than a man on his bed can hinder the growing dawn, which fills his room with brightness, and reveals to him roses outside his window.

My journey ended, as I sat at evening on a stile, these verses, I had some time before made, came into my mind :—

THE FIVE FLOWERS.

" Look, love, on your bosom
    Are flowers five :
But one has droop'd its head—
    Four alone live."

" So, late, in our nursery
    Were children five;
One rests in grassy darkness—
    Four alone live."

" Your four flowers bloom freshly, love ;
    The fifth, not as they—
Its colour, and form, and odour,
    Have passed away.
Take, then, from your bosom
    The withered one :
Can the air now nourish it ?
    Can it feel the sun ? "

" I have bound the five together
    With a fresh willow leaf,
That grew large by a river,
    As by flowing love, grief;
And they all will fall asunder
    If I loose the tie;
So a love-clasp for living babes
    Is a dead one's memory."

" Let the five flowers in your bosom, love,
    Its sweet shelter share;
As bound in one, within your heart,
    Our five darlings are.
The dead make the living dearer;
    And we will joy the more,
That the Giver, who has taken one,
    Has left us four."

Meadows were before me, sheep-dotted; a woody hill beyond; the spires and factories of a town to my right and behind me; and on my left a valley, through which there frequently shot rapid trains. Too readily, I thought, we say, We are "past feeling." The breaking up of the cloudy weather comes in due time, and mellow days succeed, with a soft, spiritual wind. We have not lost feeling because we do not feel. The numbed hand is yet alive. To-day, we care not for cream or strawberries; but to-morrow, bread may be to our revived appetite better than honey. A great sorrow that makes us weep an overrunning flood, leaves our wasted heart a desert, hard, scarred, and dry. Yet afterwards it seems to us that the sorrow made our heart to break, as an earthquake a rock, that springs of water might issue, to follow us in our wanderings through life.

As I sat thus musing, I watched the people passing along a frequented path, not far from me. They seemed of many sorts: the sinner and the meek, the widowed and the bridely; black heads, and silver heads, and auburn heads; stout youths, and ringleted maidens, and shouting children; brows cloudy, and merry, and bold, and mild, and sad. These, thought I, are, or have been, or will be, "past feeling." How many desires we outlive! They burn out, like fires: but for awhile the ashes remain hot and bright; and even afterwards these ashes are serviceable, improving the soil of our fields of character. We become dead to much while alive; and yet nothing of us truly dies, any more than we ourselves do. In regard to special days of our life, what wonderful power, too, we have of resurrection! It is allowable necromancy to consult the spirit of dead days. We question them, and they prophesy. But if they were neglected prophets while they lived, they may utter woeful prophecies when we raise them.

How many there are who wish they were " past feeling "—past the recurrence of vexed and angered, and apprehensive moods! The wise more and more become so; ruling their moods as the ship rules the waves. As the waves to the ship, so are his passions to man; he needs them, and yet they are his danger. His duty and his honour are to use them, and to rule them, and by means of them get beyond them. The wicked are " past feeling " as well as the wise; but how differently! They turn now from the pure, as swine from violets; they cast away the pearl, Truth, as if it were a pebble. Let Love speak in their ear, and they despise the music of his wisdom. They feel not when the trumpet calls to them, " Come up hither," or " Gird yourselves for battle." They know not that they are miserable and naked; and yet of one of these, wonderful is it, when the soul comes to itself, as it sometimes does, and finds itself on the wayside, wounded and bleeding; or comes home, and finds its house burned, and its garden full of thorns and nettles; then are there depths and swellings of human emotion that fill us with awe, like the ravines of mountains, or cross-seas in storms.

It were as well to be the dead or the wicked as to be the wise, if these gave away their heart, their love, their pity and aspiration, in exchange for a proud, cold wisdom. They do not so, but seek the great peace those may have whom nothing fretfully offends; desiring to rejoice with a joy unspeakable and hidden, as well as with a joy speakable and manifest. We are wise when no longer feathers tossed by the wind; but hills, steady against it, and affording shelter from it.

I continued, adds Theophilus, till dusk, watching the people and musing, and then walked back into the town; with the wakened feeling, that there was yet much for me to do, and to do hopefully, in the world. Something of my heart's thought is expressed in these verses :—

THE WORLD.

Without hills around,
Cannot be valley found
   Solitary and still;
To inclose valleys low,
   Must rise many a hill;
On which winds blow,
Whence streams flow,
   Pure and free;
And often will the hill-tops brighten'd be.

Can there then be one
Valley alone
    Named " Valley of Tears;"
Round which solitary
    No hill uprears;
Towards heaven high,
Clothed with beauty,
    Having wind and streams:
And peaks cloud-haunted from which sun-light beams?

Many hills of Hope,
With weather-fronting top,
    Around this valley are;
    Having slope and steep,
Spaces flower'd and bare;
    Clinb, do not weep,
    Nor for ease of pain sleep;
When mounted high,
Lands beyond beautiful thou shalt descry,
And the valley will seem sacred to the down-gazing eye.

FAITH AND OVERCOMING.

The day of spiritual devotement, of heartfelt
delight in God, is not gone by. Religion is not
a mere antiquity, and the Bible a sort of Tadmor
in the desert, upon which we may gaze wonder-
ingly; but with the knowledge that the old
times of greatness are gone—the greatness with

the times. We, who are but of yesterday, are as newly and truly from heaven, as Adam in Eden. The light is very old, but the morning very new. The springing of the dawn to-day is as fresh as when Eve went forth to her flowers, or Abraham to survey and tend his flocks and herds, or David sang songs to the music of his harp, or Paul rose refreshed for his zealous labours. If history is a cemetery, a sleeping-place of the ancient brave, it is also a temple where in sculptures are represented their forms and countenances, that we beholding may kindle and take courage. If our life is to be an over-coming, we must fight as to music. For spiritual earnestness to be forceful and regular, we must have assurance of principal truths, that are first, and always first. But our greatest things, though done in truth and for truth, are not done by calculation; we require a wind-like, a tidal emotion, and work best when we work as to music. There is in man a desire to be in fulness himself—to be all that he can—to live his very highest, and to have the joy of ripest, strongest being. He feels as a river-channel hollowed for the flow and rush of waters, and wants a religion with influences that shall be to his heart as a rain-power to fill it. It is by a loving faith that he may become thus strong and replenished. In love, losing ourselves we find ourselves; and it is proved to us that self-blessedness is best realized by self-abandonment. And faith is the losing of self-trust to find it. It is not the negation of our own power, but its perfecting, by true relation to a higher. We become more ourselves when we cease to depend upon ourselves. "Truth is strongest," and it is by vital connexion with truth that we become partakers of an overcoming life. He who was "the Truth" overcame, and says to us, with power as of organ-music, "Be of good cheer." But He who was the Truth was Love. It is by loving faith—faith and love blended—faith that worketh by love as its quickening life —love that has through faith assurance, a method and an object of work, that we become partakers of the Christian, the true overcoming life. The course of the world is one, though the ages are many; the life of the human race is one, though men are an innumerable multitude; and the world's life and our own are for overcoming. Good must be by conquest obtained. But what hope can there be for the creature but in a "faithful Creator"? If God has put in hazard man's good—subjected creation to evil—

only as He wars with man, only as man is assured and inspired by His Presence, can there be
overcoming. Now Christ examples the spirit of
the overcoming life which age after age strives
variously with partial but real successes. He is
God come down to fight with us and for us; He
has that spirit without measure, which we in our
measure having, overcome by. He alone who
abides in this overcoming life, his right desires
and purposes invigorated thereby, wars the best
warfare. He finds himself in his Lord. They
who have never known Christ, the " Word" of
truth and victory made flesh, have yet, so far as
they were of the truth, been of this eternal
"Word;" and so unconsciously, but most really,
of the Christ. Whoever has heartily done well,
has done more than he knew of: God had meaning and purpose in him. He was a weapon as
well as a warrior.

In some way or other we are all contending
against the world. Though the earth is fruitful,
it is stubborn; we must till the ground, conquer
the waves, and labour even to weariness for our
good. We develope the resources of the world,
and mature and discipline our own powers, by
endeavour. To get also place and right relations to our fellow-men, there must be an over-

coming. But the " good fight of faith" is especially the fight against the " present *evil* world." And as the "new man" and "old man," the good heart and the wayward and stubborn, are real, and contend in one breast, so the evil world and the good are both now with us. Full subjugation of evil is for the end ; but there is real conquest now ; there are spoils that may now be won and enjoyed, and there are times of peace in the midst of the war. Now there may be much joy where the deepest thoughts are not the most present and influential. But there cannot be earnest and exhilarating religion for powerful hearts and heads, unless there be real, we say not full, intuition of the Best and the Worst, and their relations. Then life is seen to be a painful, but sure overcoming of evil by good. Then, though endurance may need to be as that of one who, dulled and numbed, encounters for long hours a snowy wind upon the hills; yet of the good fight, notwithstanding dulness, faintings, and even discontents and hours of unbelief, it may be said that it is fought as to music. If to redeem a world mean, to bring a world, in all its provinces of action and experience confused and evil, by rightness to good, then He who creates can alone redeem.

And if the story of a world of souls, as the building plan of the earth they dwell in, is but as one thought to God, then the principles and spirit of the overcoming life have simpleness and unity; and if these be exampled in the Son of God, and exercised in fight by Him, then His history is the great analogon to which we bring the things of the earth, before and since, for spiritual comparisons; as His act is the great victorious blow by which the Spirit of truth works faith in Him, and in His assurance of conquest, and which is both cause and pledge of general victory. When it shall be said in that better country, which is not alone as sweet refreshment after earthly weariness, but also as glorious issue out of afflictions of long battle, Who hath wrought this salvation? may the world answer—I? Yes; though it shall answer too, and with adoring worship, "Thy right hand, O Lord, Thy holy arm hath gotten Thee the victory." Each answer is in its sense true—so true, that without it were true the other could not be so. Only through the consenting, hearty endeavour of men, does God work out His good plan for them—only by originating and ever-aiding Divine Love, could the world work out in patience its hopeful endeavour. God is all, but also in all.

TRUTH.

Upon a lake broad and still,
  Beneath a summer sky,
    Tones of music
Are sounding cheerfully;
  Many hearts are glad,
Praising the melody;
  Many vessels
Sweep on peacefully. `

Clouds of gloom up-gather
  In the darkening air;
Battling wind and thunders
  Fill the broad heavens fair.
·Fearfully roll the waters—
  None for music care;
Can melodies still terror?
  Soothe despair?

See man to Truth's voice listening
  As to music on still lakes;
Most rich, most various
  The melodies it makes:
In the vessel of his spirit
  Each sail gently shakes;
All the joy and hope within him
  Into full life wakes.

But the quiet time-breeze changing,
  Becomes a furious wind;
Gathering mist and darkness
  Shadow all his mind.

Danger's lightnings glare upon him—
   He is deaf, is blind;
Let the music cease; his agony,
   Can it comfort find?

Woe to man, who of Truth seeking,
   Asks alone for melody;
What he loves on quiet waters,
   He will hate with dangers nigh:
Truth, a mighty trumpet ringing,
   Sounds for war and victory;
Life on earth is for a battle—
   Not for rest or revelry.

Came from the city to-day along a thronged highway of men, felt the scene wildly wonderful, and repeated to myself with strange, serious exhilaration, my hymn called "Truth." I, as it were, shouted it aloud, though it was in the silence of my spirit. There are hours when truth gives us solemn, quieting music—nay, invites us as to pleasure music with a banquet of wine; but the thought expressed in my verses, that he who hears well, hears to be aroused, not just to be delighted, was what I felt. How wonderful all the order and tumult, the din and yet the stedfast strength, of a great city are! There the Protean human heart most variously displays itself. If the fulness of all bread were but as the fulness of hunger, and the fulness of goodness as that of knowledge and skill! It is like the sea when the four winds of heaven wrestle upon it, so that the waves roar and are troubled. But there is a King mightier than the noise of many waters. Here are hard hearts clothed in soft apparel; here is manhood girt in sackcloth. Here are the burdened, who in strong, elastic life move on unfriended yet befriending. Here are the nobly striving, whose work has been rewarded; conspicuous exhibitions of human worth and sense, fruitful trees of a wide shadow. Here the ruined and doomed have found a hell—a hell in which there are those who sport like demons with the horrid fires of passion, that burn and glow in the thick obscurities of city life, while others sit very still and moan very sorely. But with all that there is to disturb and affright us, how much is there to enliven and enlarge our heart's love and hope! Fond as man is of sight-seeing, Life is the great show for every man—the show always wonderful and new to the thoughtful. The silent country, so prosperous-looking and sacred, is glorious, but so is the city, full of men and of stirs—we delight our-

selves in the country with the abundance of peace, and in the city with the abundance of life, of human souls and labours. What cares and joys and changes are evidenced to us as the people pass us along the crowded streets! How much sin, and hope, and vehement endeavour! "One generation passeth away and another cometh, but the earth remaineth." Here are youth and age still in their glory and their beauty, as in earliest times. The rich and the poor, the good and the base, still meet together; and the same pure eyes—the eyes of the Lord —still behold the populous city and the quiet country; in each, every plant that He has not planted shall be plucked up or shall wither. And as for those that are of His right hand's planting, these shall surely have increase and perfecting.

It was getting quite dusk as I neared home. My mood had changed as I left behind me the throng of the city. I had been thinking: Wit and work are the two wheels of the world's chariot; they need to be equal, and each fixed fast. But now the fires shining through the unclosed windows, and the pleasant glimpses of domestic scenes within, filled me with new feel ing, and led to new thought. One room espe-

L

cially arrested my eye and heart. There sat in
it a girl laughing heartily—the fire-light shone
on her merry and, as they seemed, handsome
features. "You seem, dear girl," thought I, "gay
and innocent: there you sit, happy at least for
the hour, while outside your window may pass
women young as yourself, their dress squalid,
their natural grace already wasted with vice or
pain—their lot perhaps never such as yours, nor
ever to be such—and yet you,—how know I
what is within you and around you and before
you? This half-hour's mirth may be but as a
wind that cometh not soon again. But I would
rather suppose you happy, and your life hopeful and good—then you are an 'elect lady;' you
may make a 'sunshine' in many 'shady' places.
Pursue your work, and may you prosper: your
happy face will often be excellent medicine;
your word and laugh a restorative cordial for
worn spirits." A well-clad woman in a well fur-
nished room is a sight right pleasant to see ; yet
a shrunken form in a bare dwelling may be the
environment of a soul that suits by correspondence the dress and furnishings, the graceful and
free life of the lady. *May be,* I say: not all the
first are last ; but many are, and many of the
last first. A beautiful external life symbolizes

a beautiful internal life, even if such life be absent. It stands for a reality that exists somewhere. The marble bust of a woman is beautiful, though the marble be cold and dead ; and though it may not represent actual living grace, yet the living heart of woman must have given expression to living features, to make this bust possible. To create the beautiful forms and fashions of social life, how much human loveliness and intelligence have had being and activity! And though circumstance and cash may put around some of us a show of life to which we have no interior relation, and which therefore tells nothing of us ; yet this show has a most real significance concerning human qualities and delights, and even to us it gives some semblance of possessing these. Beautiful things are suggestive of a purer and higher life, and fill us with a mingled love and fear, They have a graciousness that wins us, and an excellence to which we involuntarily do reverence. If you are poor, yet pure and modestly aspiring, keep a vase of flowers on your table, and they will help to maintain your dignity, and secure for you consideration and delicacy of behaviour.

"Money is a defence, and wisdom is a defence," and, I will add, cheerfulness is a defence.

Whether my laughing lady had defence of wisdom, I know not ; but she appeared to have both defence of money and of cheerfulness. " Money is a defence." Many true things we unbelievingly say ; as, That the man is more than his coin or clothing. Many we say cantingly or inconsiderately ; as when we ask, What matter whether we be prosperous or poor ; for the rich are not therefore happy, nor the poor miserable? Facts are the ore, and truth the metal, and cant the scum. It is a Fact, that outward good is very unequally distributed. It is a Truth, that not mere things and circumstances determine happiness ; but what the man is—his tempers, and sensibility, and capacity, and religion. Yet is it Cant, to speak without discrimination of the slender purse, and sordid, limiting circumstance as inconsiderable matters. They are harassment and soreness of the bones. Soreness when we sit ; hinderance when we move. Green fields are green and inspiring, though the man who dwells among them may walk in them with careless eye and the heart of an animal; and a desert is a desert, though he who wanders over it finds its water-melons the most refreshing of fruits, and with joy and thankfulness says so.

Snow was beginning to fall as I reached home.

I sat down to the piano whilst the kettle was hissing preparation, fluttered for a minute or two over the keys, and then played Purcell's frost piece from " King Arthur," with winter comfort in my heart.

WINTER.

A first snow-flake from the sky,
　　Like a first violet of spring,
Trembling downwards loiteringly,
　　Heart delight can with it bring;
And beautiful is snow to see,
As the blossom of the apple-tree.

On mornings chilly-blue but fair,
　　When footsteps on the frost-clean ground,
Through the spirit-freshening air
　　Ringing echo all around;　.
With winter joy the households come
To the comfortable breakfast-room.

As falls the night, the waters freeze,
　　Icy fibres shoot slow;
Soon the tall and silent trees
　　In the dusk like spectres show;
Sheeted by winter power in white
A hazy robe of frost-work light.

The sunset has its winter charm,
   A glowing tint of ruddy brown;
While birds with joy and effort warm,
   As sinks the western brightness down,
The skeleton woods with gladnes fill,
Loud chirping in the twilight still.

And music-spirits black and white,
   Evoked by power of skilful fingers,
Guide into regions of delight,
   Where stillthe bloomof summer lingers;
When at evening lamps are found
Shedding domestic moonlight round.

To the city, labyrinth of homes,
   Where thepeople many-hearted dwells;
Various winter pleasure comes,
   And beautiful as summer dells
Are rooms where, in warmth and ease,
Gather friends and families.

Beauty its own has Desolation,
   Yet welcome is the spring's return;
To the strong a joy is in privation,
   Yet soon for change the heart will yearn;
And to the joyless, love must bring
In winter comfort of the spring.

CHAPTER VIII.

OH, lift your eyes unto the evermore silent heaven, that great deep, upon the breadth of whose glory may be written, "Not in word, but in mighty power!" When the curtain of the day is removed, then is unveiled this hieroglyph of eternity. There is not an evil eye among all these firmamental thousands. Sublime is the great world's azure dwelling-tent, and who is he that may tie a thread round that blue heaven, and contract it into a covering for him and for his only? It is for all the peoples of the earth. But sublimer than the day is the night, for it is the encampment of the great travelling company of worlds. The blue of day shall image for us the amplitude of the Divine charity; the night with its depth of depths shall image the vastness of the Divine wisdom. Every star mocks us if we be not immortal—but immortal we are; stars do but shame us, as with the kind look of the wise, if we regard not our immortality. But we have greater witness of immortality than that of stars —we have "that eternal life which was with the Father, and was manifested unto us." He spake not of stars, though heralded by one, and Himself called the Morning Star. The deeps of the heart and not of the heavens He unveiled; was of the earth, though not earthy; brought to us for our home human life, the Divine gift and command; came to Emmanuelize all our life; and was and remains a golden sunlight for the present, and not alone a starry glimpse of the wonderful future. Yet it is He who speaks of the Father's house of many mansions. In Him is the double promise of the life that is, and that will be. And how has the "word of the truth of the Gospel" taken as living seed such deep root, and become a tree of such a mighty shadowing shroud, but because it brings forth leaves and fruit both for health and for immortality? Slowly through vicissitude the improving course of the world advances. Each generation may take up the word, "We see not yet all things put under Him;" but each also the word, "He abideth for ever." What voice but that of Christianity proclaims immortality with a great

and calm assurance? Many voices affirm it, or
hint it, but Christianity illustriously exhibits it.
In the name of the risen Christ it proclaims the
rising of men, showing the golden key in its
hand with which it has itself opened the gates of
the grave. We have not then "infinite faculty,"
and a finite life; are not to look forth with keen
eye into the illimitable firmament, and long to
traverse it, self-poised with strong wing, and our
desire be vain. The God of stars is the God of
souls.

> Stars are for souls; but each for Him
> Abideth bright or groweth dim:
> One voice did both to being call,
> Each, self-consumed and changed, may fall.
> But souls may brightly happy be,
> Unfading through eternity;
> While stars, in courses ever new,
> Come and go like drops of dew.

HYMN AT DARK.

O Lord! most wise, most good, most true,
  The host of stars, so large and fair,
Poised in the unfathomable blue,
  Lamps of thy distant city are;
Wherein, in many mansions rich and wide,
  Dwellers and guests discoursing rest or move;
Wherein are found the bridegroom and the bride,
  Sweet changing voices of continuing love.

Also, O Lord! most great, most strong,
    Thy distant stars are ships of flame ;
And voyaging spirits, unseen, prolong
    An unheard melody to Thy name:
Sounding it forth ever with soul-filling strain,
    Soft or most mighty, as earth's varying wind ;
They float the illimitable, stormless main,
    Wide, deep, and still, as Thine unchanging mind.

And, Lord, thou eternal, only fair,
    In hollow heaven, a valley deep,
As shining tent each fixèd star
    Doth its appointed station keep;
But tent-filled spaces thou canst change, O Lord!
    And at Thy will another heaven may be ;
As Israel moved and rested at Thy word,
    So journey spirits from nothingness to Thee.

Lord God! these solemn heavens of night,
    A darkened Vast, are like to Thee;
For every where great beams of light
    Break forth from Thine immensity;
And as waves shine when mighty vessels move,
    So Time the wave, Eternity the deep,
Shines starful, as the vessel of Thy love
    Doth in its course majestic onward sweep.

A man may see the moon rise among his own
trees, and the stars sink over his own dwelling ;
and so may spiritual truths have to him, in his
knowledge and circumstance, their relative ap-

pearances. But other men, seeing the same moon, and stars, and sun, behold them from among their own groves and dwellings. Every where the heaven is over the earth, and every where a religious sacredness over-canopies the life of men. Yet it is what we each see, that the heaven appears to enclose; and immediately behind the limit of our vision seems the limit of the heaven. The heaven, which is over all the earth, can limit its appearance for each man's vision. We, also, should endeavour to ascend to a true thought of its vastness, as it thus condescends to our individual life. Our own way of life affords us a sensible horizon; but as we think of the life of the world, let us remember that there is a rational one also.

If our own "sanctuary" is not more sacred to us than another, because it is our own, no sanctuary will be sacred. We have one of the chapels of the great temple, and will love it; but the temple should be more to us than this chapel, or any other. Our own method of worship, or habit of life, may be to us as a cherished staff on which we have long leaned, and which we have learned to love; let us not use it as a sword, with which to vex and slay. Truth individualizes, love unites. Where there is some truth with but little love, there will be haughty isolation. Where there is some love with but little truth, there will be zealous, apprehensive bigotry. The more that Truth and Love are co-equally influential, the readier will the man whom truth individualizes be to allow and respect another's individualization; but each will regard himself individual as a branch, not as a vine—a branch also neither fully expanded nor perfectly fruitful; and individual through a dependence in common with many branches upon one source of life.

THE TWO WINDS.

Oh! how chill the weather is,
  Oh! how dreary and how dry,
When across the plains of land
  East winds coming, cloud the sky:
So coldly comes the darkening air
  From word-wastes of theology.

But Wisdom is the western wind
  That traverses Life's ancient Sea,
Its breath is very soft and mild,
  Very warm and showery:
Now blooms the heart, for now we feel
  Christ's own Christianity.

We are our fathers' heirs; and they have not alone left us their properties, but their memories. Not alone devolved on us encumbrances, but given us the story of their sins and struggles. Of all that we have thus received, the personal history and the recorded utterances of the wise and the virtuous possess the highest value. By the wisdom of former producing minds, those of the present age are strengthened and developed. We have not alone the things made and done, but the influence of the doers. Our forefathers live among us not alone by what they did, but by what they were. We can do the more greatly for what they did, only as we are the greater for what they were. All that we do depends upon what we are: he then who has left to the world the record of a noble life, though he may have left no outward memorial, has left an enduring source of inward, and, through inward, of outward greatness. A thing of nature may from its beauty inspire us with an enthusiasm that shall quicken our sensibility, and aid us in our endeavour to depict it. In a still higher manner does a good man aid us to reproduce himself. An individual of illustrious virtue manifests some general quality of life in a specific form of beauty. He breathes into us

his life, that we may exhibit new, though related forms of fair behaviour.   Thus the fathers
speaking to us no more, yet breathe on us:
away from us, they are yet among us as benefi-
cent and aidful spirits.   In the highest manner
is the Christ thus with us.   It is not so much
we, that with careful skill and patient industry
model ourselves after Him, as He that, as we
gaze, more and yet more transforms us.   Christian carefulness and industry we exercise, but
these may best be represented as a gaze into the
beaming, intelligent face of human religion,
which is Christ; and as a communion with its
warm pure heart, which is Christ also.   There
have been in our world many kinds of great
men.   Philosophers and heroes, wise men who
have kindled lamps in darkness, men of power
who have quelled the tumult of the people;
some who have braved with forehead of flint
public attack; others who have with patience
suffered—greatly, but in retirement.   Many as
have been these forms of excellence, they have
yet all been partial or blemished; but the excellence of Christ was not such—it was not for
classes, but for man—not for an era, but for all
time.   It was goodness in its grandest, purest,
most elementary forms, not alone perfect of its

kind, but perfect as the great life and supporting basis of all kinds.

The men of the past live for us in their examples, but live for us, so far as we know, with but
partial and occasional consciousness of what we
are and want. We love them, and may feel
that they could have loved us. But the Christ,
living, knows how we need and are affected by
the record of His life on earth. Not only did He
bear griefs in such way that we, considering His
history, are helped to bear ours; but we may
feel that the heart and mind which thus did and
endured, have knowledge of us, and sympathiz-
ing communion with us. We must identify God
and Christ. If we say, "Thou God seest us," it
is as if we said, "Thou Christ seest us." God
becomes Christ when He looks upon us in our
human weakness and endeavour. We are not
left to imagine how our Saviour would have felt,
but to represent to ourselves how He does feel.
Christ's truths are the eyes of God looking on
us; His love, the heart that fills those eyes with
kind and brightest light. God becomes a man
for men, lives ever as a man for them; He is
Christ to them. Our fathers may have suffered
for conscience' sake, have endured with a meek
but unfearing firmness, have suffered in body,

yet rejoiced in spirit—they are gone. We are strengthened both to bear and to act by intercourse with their memories; we are wrought on and encouraged, as if they were witnesses of our action and deportment—yet they are gone. We cannot tell what they know of us and our struggles—we have no hope of help from them. But our Saviour lives: He is with God, and is God. God who knows all, through Him sees all, and according to Him orders all. He sends forth the spirit of His Son to encourage and guide. By that spirit were the men strengthened whose finished course encourages us, and we may receive effectual strength, so that we too shall encourage others. We who live now, live that we may work for God and for His Christ. All times are wonderful—we may, however, so speak of times as if we imagined we were but spectators. But if there be evil, let us remember that we are not looking at a tragedy, that we may bewail over it—but living in a time of difficulty, that we may work. The character of the age and our own character have relation. All necessary influence of the age upon us is known and considered; but our influence upon the age, though it may be inappreciable, is real, and, so far as our efforts will avail to change its

character, we are responsible for its being what
it is. Neither this, nor any other responsibility,
can we exactly measure. It is never said to us
—So much thou owest—this is the exact sum;
but it is said—In this way it behoves thee to
work, do what thou canst, and that heartily.
Often, hidden thoughts, when they come into
the free atmosphere of action, swell into great
giants, terrible to the wicked, but mightily helpful to the good. But though there may be in us
no such thoughts, yet is not our work worthless.
The greater part of the goodness at any time
in the world, is the goodness of common character. The chief part of the good work done
must be done by the multitude. In all times
there have been leaders; but these great men
gathered round them companies, growing gradually to great armies. We look back to former times and the struggles that then were, and
wish we had been helpers in the fight: but there
is honourable warfare now, and if we see not
what must be done now, or have not the courage
to do it if we can see, neither should we have
had vision or courage then.

Speaking after the manner of men:—How
daringly does God manage the world! How
can he—how will he, solve the doubts and

M

satisfy the yearnings of all the good, and make the saved world see of the travail of its soul with full satisfaction? We cannot wonder at the greatly wrong yet powerful contrast, of God and Devil, as two ever-striving, nigh co-equal powers of good and evil, that has risen from the perplexed thought and imagining of the world. A God who does only good, and all the good He can—a Devil who does only evil, that mightily, and sometimes with the advantage. The Christian thought of one God, the Good, who is supreme; with also a real and opposed, but limited power of Evil, is far higher and nobler than this, though of far more difficult attainment for the world. He who ordains trial by sin, who suffers Time with its dark wings to brood over the human heart devouringly, has in His Son uttered a voice of mercy for man, which is a voice of doom for evil; He most powerfully controls all evil influences, and will bring on after the night of sorrows a morning so glorious, that powers of heavenly vision must be prepared for the outbreak of heavenly light. Christianity enables us to make distinction between Divine evil and diabolic evil—a distinction which may remain clear and valuable in thought, when, in a great mixed case of fact, we cannot at once or at all see how far sin is working in hatred, and how far wisdom darkly working in love. Essential evil is—Sin ; spirit and life against the Divine spirit and life—its fruits are miseries many. That souls may be of free choice and with full joy dependently one with God, great schemes of sorrowful experiences are devised : all designed to give full proof to the worlds of what is evil, and of what evil is, and to exert over evil for those who freely by aidance become " partakers of the Divine nature," influences that shall control and destroy it. Evil in the diabolic sense is life consciously opposed to the Divine life.

But evil that we will call Divine, is the defect and suffering constituted for the disciplinatory development of individuals and worlds, who, if to be made partakers of Divine delight, must become consciously partakers of the Divine thought and will. Only that is diabolic evil which is consciously opposed to the Divine life. But in the widest sense : Whatsoever is opposite to God is evil ; pains may be therefore so called, because they are opposed as experiences to the Good, which as felt is Joy, as thought is Truth, as done is Right. But the Divine work in painfulness is against pain, by being against

error and wrong. The diabolic work even in
pleasure is towards pain and death, because according to error and wrong. Pains ordained in
wisdom for good are in the lightest sense evil.
Spirit and life against the Divine spirit and life
—though knowing this not at all, or knowing it
imperfectly—are in a higher sense evil. But in
the most restricted and empathic sense, that is
evil which is consciously opposed to God. With
an evil consciousness is necessarily associated
life evil beyond consciousness, and the life
tends to complete oppositeness to God—it is
diabolic.

The humanity of the world is evil, as actually
opposed to God; but not universally evil, as consciously opposed to Him. We are born into a
naturalness which we must discover to be evil,
constituted to be so born; such naturalness of
each individual man is his evil divinely ordained.
When as evil it is revealed to him, and he
decides to oppose it; he knows his nature as
wicked by himself becoming holy, devoted to
the good. If he yields himself to the life opposed
to the Divine, seeing it to be so opposed, he sins,
and is so far partaker of the essential evil life.
Nature, then, as evil, is the life unconsciously
opposed to God. The Diabolic is the life con-

sciously so opposed. There is a sense, then, in which the devil is the soul of nature—the evil Spirit in the evil Life. The great Divine scheme is the overcoming evil by good; and in this scheme, voluntary and involuntary experiences of suffering are made the great instruments by which good contends and conquers; so that good, by evil as Suffering, overcomes evil as Sin, and for this warfare worlds are constituted to be born into evil as Disorder.

In the overthrowing of sin, good and evil are both made known, and thus the highest blessedness possible realized for free and conscious beings in communion with God and with one another. The Spirit of the Son is sent abroad into the earth, the spirit of patient, sacrificing love. He suffered to hinder suffering, died that a sacrificing spirit might go forth and prevail against "him who hath the power of death—the devil." Involuntary sufferings are ordained for our perfecting in strength, in trust, in love for one another; but it is as these sufferings, as well as those freely undertaken in the spirit of sacrificing love, are in that spirit borne, that they become sacred and salutary, full of blessings and of hopes. God is our Father and the world's Father. He looks into the far depths of our soul and the world's, and into the far future. He discerns all possible unfoldings of the heart, all issues of event and discipline. It is not simply ourself, this man or another, that is in probation; it is a world that is in probation. The heavenly Father regards the highest welfare of the whole family. Let us believe in a plan for the world, no matter that we cannot understand it, and that the Divine methods with the individual must depend upon this plan for the race. Then it will be enough as to Well-being, that we can ascertain its governing spiritual condition. Painful things may come on us, because of what is good for the brotherhood. If, then, we would interpret these, we must study the laws of general welfare; and if, though unable to interpret, as must often happen, we would feel trust and thankfulness, there must be in us brotherly kindness as well as filial obedience. Personal experience will often reveal to us the great laws that govern that of the world, and then these laws, as such, become to us guarantee for the good issue of our own experience. Whatever discipline of pain or toil affects individuals, is on a gigantic scale, and in ten thousand instances working in the world. The saved companies of heaven will be glorious and happy societies of proved men ; not forming

an aggregate of individuals, delivered and prepared by separate disciplines, but a great spiritual community, saved by a system of disciplines
—disciplines infinite in number, yet all related;
so causing each individual to be bound to others
and to the community by strongest cords of love,
experiences and affections wonderfully interwoven.

Longing for the heaven, if there be no yearn-
ing and endeavour for present pureness of life
and inward sacred peace, may be a striving to
"feed upon the wind," when nothing substantial-
seeming is at hand; but cannot be more. And
outcry with congratulation about "the good time
coming," if there be no heavenliness, no belief in
eternal thoughts, which only with grand slowness
fulfil themselves, can be but an eager, sanguine
lust—never a solemn, inspiring hope. Let the
"good time" we desire on earth be a heavenly
time, and the heaven we look for be one that
may now begin in the heart. Then while
working, as we hope and quietly wait, we shall
sometimes sing:—

HYMN OF FAITH AND HOPE.

Maker of worlds! of spirits Father!
  Hear Thou our utterance!
    We live from Thee:
And this to know and feel, oh, grant us! rather
  Than that, in folly, we
  Should joy iu favouring chance,
    Or curse harsh destiny.

O God! Thy great thoughts are as mountains,
  Dark in their loftiness,
    Mist-veiled they stand;
Far up, the trading rivers have their fountains,
  The life-streams of the land;
  Discovering winds we bless,
    Which show the outline grand.

Time is a dawn, for ever brightening
  To its day of million years,
    Thou, God, the sun;
Swift as the impetuous, divided lightning
  Our vain thought hurries on;
  But to change all cloudy fears
    The gold light hath begun.

Slow, but sure-prospering her salvation,
  Earth works out mediately,
    Thy love the power;
And wisdom intricate, a fold each nation,
  Each man, and every hour,
  Is opening silently
    Smooth beauty of its flower.

Man still is dark and dead in sinning,
  Wintry his heart and life;
    But Thy Son dear,
As the mild spring-power his strong way is winning,
  The heaven of thought grows clear;
  Winds make a gusty strife,
    But buds all round appear.

The river of the peoples, onward going,
  Bright-waved, but dark below,
    Its sea-course takes;
Now rough, now still, this spirit-stream, deep-flowing,
  Strange windings makes;
  Swiftly it moves, then slow,
    Oft eddying as in lakes.

Like a fugue chorus is creation,
  Framed of proportions vast;
    Each voice is found;
And ever newly some arising nation
  Swells the great tide of sound,
  Till in oneness grand at last
    The full song shall resound.

Grant that in faith we may be willing
  At the end to be full blest;
    That patiently
Our part appointed in Thy thought fulfilling,
  Day-builded life may be
  Both temple and home of rest,
    Each finished wondrously.

CHAPTER IX.

TRINAL'S DIARIUM.

SUNDAY.

Day melts into the night,
　The night into the morning;
Darkness swallowing the light,
　Light from the dark dawning;
So melts knowledge into Mystery,
　The solemn dark of stars;
So from the Obscure arises wisdom,
　With dewy fragrant airs;
Be there for us to-day these twilights two,
That we may view,
As the earth darkens, heavenly hopes appear;
As the heaven brightens, earthly things grow clear.

MONDAY.

The Difficult, like the cocoa-nut,
　Rich milk it hath within;
Through husk and shell, by labouring well,
　An entrance you may win;

You hear the flowing of the milk
   If angrily you shake it;
But if you would the sweetness taste,
   Try patiently and break it.

TUESDAY.

Love hath the power of chemist rare,
     For into many sorrow cups
     He smiling drops
His dewy, radiant tear;
Changing into sweet and bright,
Draughts that were salt as seas, black as the night.

WEDNESDAY.

Sometimes to man is given
   A thought from heaven!
Coming softly, as the falling snow
   Comes from the skies;
And resting pure upon the silent spirit
   As on the earth snow lies;
But quickly as the snow in spring
   It passes away:
And the heart darkens as the ground
   Where the whiteness lay.

THURSDAY.

Seek thou thy God alone by prayer,
   And thou wilt doubt, perhaps despair;
But seek Him also by endeavour,
   And gracious thou wilt find Him ever.

Seek thou thy God alone by work,
   Aud prospering, thou wilt not bless;
For pride will in thy doings lurk,
   And in thine heart unthankfulness.

FRIDAY.

My wish was a bubble
   Large and fair;
Coloured and bright, but hollow and light,
   It burst with a breath, and vanished in air.
My hope was a flower
   Large and fair;
The winds blew rough, the blossom fell off,
   But slowly and securely a fruit grew there.

SATURDAY.

Our spirit is a temple, and a home,
   Time is for worship, and a time for mirth:
Honrs solemn and sportive may to each man come,
   Earth loves the heaven, and the heaven loves earth.
Firesides as firmaments are Divine, for One
Kindles a log-blaze and the glorious sun;
Gabriel, perhaps, when he from toil reposes,
White-winged disports himself, becrown'd with roses.

PRIVATE JUDGMENT.

The world, which we may see and examine, is
very various and complex. There are the seas,

the firmament, the great mountains, the wonders
that the earth embowels, the living creatures in
all their number and diversity. Science presents
to man her book—but he is free. Has he not
eyes, and hands, and his own powers of thought?
Is not the world before him? The book of
science records how other men have observed
and meditated; but has he not his right of
private judgment—may he not try to find out
the world for himself? Certainly ; he may do
what he will, and—what he can. What he will
must be limited by what he can. And the like
right of private judgment, with the like limitation,
a man has in regard to the Bible, which is the
foundation book of wisdom; and in regard to
the other books of wisdom of the different ages,
which are therewith truly connected, though their
connexion may not be recognized, nor its law of
relation truly expressed. Our eyes may be as
clear, and all our hungerings as new and original,
as those of Adam. Our faculties of thought
may be as real and efficient, according to kind
and measure, as those of Plato or Shakspeare.
But the times in their course have unfolded
much; and these wiser ones of mankind have
recorded in weighty words the visions and pon-
derings of their hearts. And upon our Bible we

may write—"Thou shalt rise up before the hoary
head." The eye of this sage is not dim, nor his
natural force abated ; his brow is grave as with a
burden of still unuttered truth; his yet youthful
eye is bright as with a new-fallen tear of mercy.
We may exercise our thought upon God, and
religion, and human well-being, and the whole
wide world of spiritual realities. We have our
private judgment, and may do what we can;
and what we can do we are bound to do. Our
eyes must themselves see, what yet without
direction they would not have learned to observe;
our mind, by its own effort, must apprehend
truth, that by that effort it could not have discovered. Neither individuals nor communities
may safely assert the right of private judgment,
unless the duty of private judgment is weightily
felt. When a thinking man feels bound to be a
reality—bound to learn of truth and obey truth
—then he feels his limitation ; and claiming his
right, that he may perform his duty, in all lowli-
ness and earnestness of spirit he exercises his
faculty of inquiry. Our limitation is real; but
so is our faculty real. Folly forbids inquiry
because of limitation, and then establishes dark
tyranny; or renounces inquiry because of limitation, and then sinks into thick, unwholesome

mists of ignorance. Wisdom declares us not wholly dependent, nor wholly independent, but inter-dependent—having real powers, limited according to laws that gradually become defined and clear, as we advance onward in a modest and communing spirit.

TIME.

Wonderful, solemn, all-changing time, that which creates and destroys, ripens and devours, blights and embellishes! Time is a flowing river, wide as a sea; from it arise bubbles that burst, huge misty spectres that dissolve, structures that shape themselves upon the dark waters, and grow as they float. The eras are as garments clothing the eternal thoughts as they develope themselves and grow up in the world : in a succession of such enlarging vestures, each growing thought is apparelled. And the whole time of the earth is an ocean, a fathomless but limited portion of the great deep of eternity.

THE SEA AND THE RAINS.

Fresh-water rains
　Come from the salt and bitter sea;
And the sunny shower
　Was once a dark wave heaving stormily.

Vast spreading Time,
　Is a wind-aroused unshelter'd ocean;
Wave following wave
　Of bitter and dark Event in endless motion.

But the saltness gone
　High in our spirit as the air,
Ascending mists
　Into the clouds of thought collected are.

Then fall fresh showers
　Upon all plains, all mountain-tops;
Pure uttered words,
　Many, electric, large as summer drops.

And new clouds ever,
　To wander are rising from this sea;
With a blessing stored,
　Rich influence of truth and poetry.

And the heart possessing
　Its power of purpose and of deed;
This sweet from bitter
　Wakens for bloom and fruit the holy seed.

In the wide sea of Time are things small and great, innumerable. Look upon the waters, and they are dark; but take of them in a crystal vessel, and the water shall be clear. Each single hour is transparent, but who can see into the depths of time? Pour back from your vessel its water into the ocean, and let your hour be numbered with the hours of eternity, and, what was before so clear, now forms part of the dark mass through which no eye can pierce, and is itself dark. Thus, also, is it with the truth and the providence of God; we know them in their parts, we know them not in their greatness. Providence is around us as the encompassing air which sustains our life. Truth, as the encompassing light which vivifies. Yet is our truth but as a torch in the night, and our earthly life as but breath for a day: the fulness of truth and providence is hidden in the Fulness of Time, and that fulness is Eternity.

But the Present, though it seem but as a wind which soon passes away, is yet full of wonder and greatness. For it is also a seed ripened by the Past, and in which the Future is hidden. Every Time is both a product and a cause. The infinitely varied actions of the past terminate, regarded earthwise, in the present;

N

whilst this present is as a mighty seed which
enfolds the undeveloped but embryo-existing
future. Each seed has required the plant with
all its curious apparatus; and the plant for its
growth needed sunshine, pure winds, nurturing
rains, and an appropriate soil. Words and
deeds, and days and times, are all as the seed,
which is both germ and product. From them
may much originate; and for their ripening,
continuance and change of many processes were
required. Consider a time or a truth: it is a
seed, enclosing we will say a principle, a temper,
an inquiry, as its strong and germinant life. What
diverse disciplines, joyous and sorrowful, were
needed for the nurturing of those plants—the
World and the Mind, that bore these seeds!
And if only through the persisting operation of
slow-maturing thoughts, powers, and affections,
that great seed, the Present, has been produced;
only after long and thorough working of many
influences, can it unfold the large and blossoming growth that its vitality makes possible.
The spirit of a man, and of mankind, are each
as a country fruitful in variety of plants, and thus
producing germs of many kinds. Each germ is a
product, each product a germ. And if we regard
our own nature and human nature as estates for

cultivation, then we and our race are husbandmen. Much endeavour is as clearance and drainage of wild fenny country; and sowing and reaping are ever beautiful emblems of action and result. For in sowing we take germs and submit them to influences, which as result give us at harvest germs of a like kind, but in larger quantity. The processes employed are human, the influences Divine. The latter act by occasion of the former; but where the first are, the last are sure. If we heedfully and laboriously plough and sow, though the blighted fields may be many, yet shall we and the world, after due patience, find a harvest cheering and abundant. We need ever to remember, for thankfulness and for hope, that what is now easy and natural for a man and for the world, may have become so only after many labours, and cares, and experiences. Our clearness, confidence, and love may indicate to the wise, that we have known long and weary meditation, numerous fears and fightings, many storms of doubt, many rains of sorrow. The mind when truly humanized, and the world when truly civilized, will resemble a luxuriant tropical garden-island. This island has become such after lapse of years, and succession of many processes. Soil slowly formed; seeds cast by

ideas passing as birds of the air ; living principles floated into the soul over the great sea of
experience, like fruits and animal germs on drift-
wood : thus has been formed the garden, with its
shade, sunny openings, and beauty. By nature
and by labour; by wonderful formative and
changing processes independent of us; by our
own ploughing and sowing—nature and self
alike working by Divine influences—we and the
world have arrived at our present, and shall
arrive at our future.

Here are other, but related thoughts :—The
generations do not succeed each other abruptly,
but pass one into another like the pictures in
dissolving views. It is not, strictly, one generation only that exists on earth at a given time :
because of differences in our years of life, we
are as a family of generations; because of the
different stages of national advancement, we are
a society of ages. Yet are we who live at this
hour our fathers' heirs, and a great inheritance
they have left us ; with it have come burdens
and embarrassments, yet is it great. The state
of society at any given period, is the development of that sum of knowledge and character
that has accumulated since man bent his intellect to the study of truth and nature, and God

began to train his spirit. We are perpetually entering iuto the labours of others, and ourselves labouring that others may enter into ours. Almost all present good is in part only achieved by us, being in part an inheritance from our forefathers. But the stream of knowledge, as it flows, both deepens and widens; it will bear upon it constructions more in number and mightier in form. To the prosperity and civilization of our time all past times have contributed; individuals may work for themselves, but communities work for the world. The prosperity of our time! Is there not evil? Alas! enough. Society a development of knowledge and character? Say, rather, of ignorance and wickedness! No, we will not forget the evil, but neither will we forget the good. The childhood and youth of the world have not been "vanity" —though by many vanities and sins they have been hurt and disfigured. Every time brings its own good and evil. Many of those classes that specially enjoy the good, will see the evil indistinctly; many of those who specially suffer the evil, will see the good indistinctly. Thus, at all times, there will be two different, yet not necessarily opposed tendencies—the tendency of the conservative, and that of the advancing. We shall see—let us not quietly see—aged error, with its withered fingers, strangling young truth in its robust infancy; and we shall see—let it not again be quietly, and with approval—hasty and angry discontent, with its axe laid to the root of the old stocks of good, busy in destroying trees of life, that need only free air and wise pruning in order to yield the desired abundance.

There is much novelty that is without hope, much antiquity without sacredness.' Spiritual wisdom is for the old and the new a reconciling power; it knows that the old and the new are each necessary, each insufficient; that a regard for the old fixes and deepens individual and national character, and a regard for the new enlivens and advances these. It knows that roots are the best friends of boughs and blossoms; and that the still-spreading width and ever-renewing beauty of these are the true glory of the roots. Wisdom knows that the youth of a time uttering its voice against grievance and corruption, is as the hand of God writing in letters of fire upon the palace of established custom, the very timbers of which may cry out of oppressions,—Thou art wanting, and art doomed. But wisdom knows also that the course of the world is as the setting in of a tide that has not yet reached high water,—that each new wave advances with raised front, falls forward with a dash, and goes on to its limit,—then lastly, retiring a little, over it the next wave advances, and in like manner falls, goes on to its limit, and retires. The old is partly as the Trunk of the tree, which has through a thousand summers been building itself up, and partly as the Life of the tree, which examples its powers newly each spring, as it has a thousand times exampled them before. The new is partly as the Budding of the tree, and partly as the Spring Influences that expand and beautify the tree ; and without which the trunk, however vast, would serve only for burning, or as a monumental pillar to its own departed life. The spirit of love is that which renews in hope both our life and the world's. It makes all things new ; and, so far as the endeavouring spirit of an age is a loving one, the thoughts find application that rise in the heart as it meditates on—

LOVE AND SPRING.

The black trees shall green clothing have,
Upon the dark lands corn shall wave,
And rain from the bright clouds of spring
Beauty of budding life shall bring ;

The heaven put on change of blue,
The earth be garmented anew,
And thus the mild and virgin year
Be clad in maiden-raiment fair;
Then early radiance shall beam through
Myriad drops of morning dew,
And birds rejoicingly shall sing,
Ascending with sleep-freshened wing;
Bright-wall'd heaven re-echoing.
And soft, and sweet, and pure, and free,
As maiden's breath, the air shall be,
Hushing the soul entrancingly:
And from the hush, as birth of power,
Come Love, like wind-attended shower;
Making the heart as rain-swell'd brook,
Which narrowing limits has forsook;
When bright and varying, swift and free,
The waters stream on eddyingly.
Love can give to life the sense
Of being, thousandfold intense;
In heart and thought, as earth and air,
Create a universal stir;
With a new eye, the spirit bless
Upbeaming into boundlessness.
Laws of light may tell me why
Such colour hath the sea and sky;
But only Love explains to me,
Why I look on both delightedly.
Clear-voiced science makes me know
Of summer rains and winter snow;
Why the winds rush, the rivers flow;

But Love from waters, weather, wind,
Brings changing joy of heart and mind.
Love a triple crown shall wear,
It governs sea, and land, and air;
By triple star shall emblem'd be,
Its power, joy, eternity.
Love has sorows with delight,
Wildly clouded, lustrous-bright;
But like winter-conquering spring,
By storm advances blossoming.
When the sapphire-builded sky
Dims and totters tremblingly;
Earnest, everlasting Love,
Shall its storm-swept heaven remove.

SPRING VERSES.

I.

From vapoury folds with glorious edges,
  Liberal clouds pour forth the rain;
The plenteous gift makes bright the hedges,
  Bright the fields, and bright the plain.

The happy wind this bounty shaketh
  Down on the earth with kindly power;
And each sweet leafy smell it taketh
  To fill with healthier force the shower.

And oh! the sun in glory beaming,
   And oh! the widening wing of blue,
And oh! the hush: and oh! the gleaming
   Of the rain-drops fallen new.

And oh! the buds, and oh! the voices,
   And oh! the first white butterfly:
Our heart, so strangely it rejoices,
   Needs it must both sing and sigh.

Thousand million buds are rounding,
   Million little leaves expand;
From woody depths deep tones are sounding,
   A first flower trembles in our hand.

Life with thrill of new emotion
   Pulses to the spring-tide rule,
Like a wide, breeze-trembling ocean,
   All astir, all beautiful.

Love sways: colours are her vesture,
   Every sound, it is her voice:
Every movement is her gesture;
   Oh! rejoice with her, rejoice.

II.

Spring is but a longer morming
  For its day of summer dawning,
    Awake! Awake!
From the dark and sodden earth
  Beauty every where has birth,
    All slumbers break.

No longer roars the foaming stream,
  Like one that crieth in his dream,
    Softly it flows:
Heavy no more and dark the sky,
  The vaulted Heaven, clear and high,
    Its morning knows.

Awake! thou winter-weary heart,
  And in the general joy have part,
    Dream thou no more;
Taller and fairer every hour
  Stems uplift their folded flower,
    Dear Summer's store.

And hearts must bloom that hearts may fruit,
  Safe abides the ancient root
    Through winter's pain;
No heart so eldered by its care,
  But may anew its blossom bear
    And fruit again.

Forth-pushing with a gentle strength,
   Each new shoot of thy heart at length
     Firmly may stand :
Show thou by early love and praise—
   Feeling the force of coming days—
     Summer at hand.

Spring is but a longer morning
   For its day of summer dawning,
     Oh ! welcome day :
Morning comes, a lesser spring,
   New energy of life to bring
     Morrow ! be May.

CHAPTER X.

FLORA AND THE FLOWERS.

Oh! if the rose be hailed the queen,
   A princess is the lily,
And modest violets, I ween,
   And humble daffodilly;
The primroses and pansies fair,
   Sweet-William and the daisies,
Beautiful Flora's children are—
Their loveliness her joy and care:
     And every summer hour
     Some blooming flower
Its bright face raises,
And in its silent beauty Flora praises.

Flora! should'st thou appear
   Thy starry family among,
Upon a white cloud, on a morning clear,
   Borne by a soft wind strong;

Scarfed with the rainbow thou would'st be,
   Zoned with hue-changing mother-of-pearl;
And o'er thy forest-tinted robe
   Deep golden maiden-hair would curl;
And on thy open bosom would rest,
     Most blest,
The queen-flower, Rose;
   Giving to the beauty lily-bright,
   Hair-shadowed, as the hills by Night,
   The rosy-tinted sunset light
Of Alpine snows.

O Flora!
   Thou dost minister
   Ever in tenderness,
     Ever in truth.
To thee the flower-spirit, kindest heaven
This work of love in charge hath given,
   To adorn and to bless,
   To teach and to soothe;
And every budding, blooming flower,
   Every flower fading,
With a spiritual power
   In the work is aiding;
Whilst thou, still-faced, and with love-lighted eye,
   Apparell'd all divinely,
   Oft wandering near invisibly,
     Dost smiling watch benignly.

Whilst by a flower some heart is healed,
Or by a flower some truth revealed,
Or in a garden, wood, or field,
    Or by a stream,
Some heart loved-tranced, shadowed by visions fearful,
      Wakes from its dream,
Flower-disenchanted, to a hope-dawn cheerful.

Thee, Flora! every maiden,
   Herself a flower,
    Most warmly blesses;
Because in lonely and forsaken hour
   Thou comfortest distresses.
Full oft her heart is heavy-laden,
  As by honey stored within,
  Which none may win
But he who comes as delicately
As to a flower comes the bee.

Imogen—Una—Marion fair—
Susan, and Grace, and Eleanor—
  Louisa, Jane, and Mary—
The heaven has bless'd you every one;
Ye each have blossom of your own,
  And, like the flowers, vary.
Ye live not for yourselves alone,
  Compassionate and tender;
And even as the flowers are,
O Flora! cherished by thy care,
Of maidens delicate, and pure, and fair
  Our love shall be defender.

Flora, beautiful and wise,
Skill'd in human mysteries!
Hearts there are to hymn thy praises,
Many and lowly as the daisies—
Daisies, which embellish spring
With half-hidden blossoming.
Hearts there are, deep and pondering,
Flower-filled with love and wondering;
Every when and every where
Sweetest flowers welcome are.
At sight of some fresh-blossoming flower,
The curtain'd sick receive a power;
To him that sorroweth and striveth,
The flower-cup wine of comfort giveth;
Wine medicinal and pure,
Wine to cheerfulize and cure.
The little one, too early blest,
Hath flowers in his coffin'd rest;
New-gathered blooms their odours shed,
Sweet as the memory of the dead.
At festivals and seasons holy,
Times of mirth and melancholy;
In solitude, in joy, and care,
Sweetest flowers welcome are.
The maiden changing to the wife,
Now in the bloom-hour of her life,
Hath flowers in her hand and hair;
Flowers upon her bosom are.
Oh! gather from the rough hill-side
Some flower to adorn the bride!
It shall fade, let love endure
Strong as the hill, its flower as pure.

Like white blooms in the thick, black tresses,
'Mid fortunes dark are love's caresses,
And light or dark, as flowers with hair,
Love and life enwoven are.
When griefs, Time's roaming archery,
Scattering arrows wantonly,
Wound in unexpected hour,
Then for healing touch a flower;
Nature is the robe of God—
God the merciful and good:
Flowers are the embroider'd hem,
Virtue he hath given them;
Tremulous and blushing sorrow,
Unrebuked, may healing borrow;
Welcome as flowers, so welcome we
To the blessings of their ministry.

Flora! when the eastern flush
　　Doth the coming sun betoken,
Stillest morning's sacred hush
　　As yet all unbroken;
Dewed nourishingly, every flower
In joy awaits the hour
　　When, sun-touched, it shall brightly open.

Then, as pass the hours
Freshly work the flowers;
And ever some one, stooping sadly,
Culls an opening blossom gladly;

O

And looking long within,
    As in a glass sees there,
Something of his spirit, undefiled with sin,
And yet undimmed with care.

But different in their ministry
    These flowers of the dawn ;
For some shall grace festivity,
    Some comfort the forlorn ;
And some shall please the poor and sick,
    And some the fair adorn ;
But all shall work most lovingly,
    For therefore were they born.

The green earth hath its flower, the sky—
    That mighty flower of blue ;
And whilst it still blooms bright and high,
    Shall lesser flowers bloom too.
Work, Flora, then, rejoicingly,
    And give us blossoms new.

———————

" This poem was in part made by a river-side,
on a quiet, most summerly September day ; in
part by the kitchen fireside, where I took refuge
on the chilly evening of that day ; and in part
while walking, on a neighbour day, over and
over a wide, flat field, fringed with great trees.
That field has often been to me a field of

treasure ; and those trees, trees of life. In a wind, their noise is as the voice of a great city, or of the surge-beaten solitary shore. I have heard them whisper, as if hushing the world around to sleep ; and seen them as still as those who stand musing over a grave. I have been with them when bright as a bride ; and found them calm and immovable when wet with the winter showers."

THE TWO MAIDENS.

A little maiden light and bright
   As bubble on a river,
Declared she loved, and love she would
   For ever : yes, for ever :
But when a wind of change arose,
   And waves began to quiver,
This bubble light, although so bright,
   It melted in the river.

A maiden pure, and purer was
   No water lily ever,
Said : Time will flow, but love may grow
   And bloom anew for ever :
Her heart, like lily in the stream,
   The wild winds made it quiver ;
But as they blew, the lily grew
   And rooted in the river.

LOVE.

Oh! Love is not a nectar fine,
  With woman for the bowl,
Madly to be tossed aside
  In drunkenness of soul.

Love, it is both bread and wine,
  A sacrament of hearts;
And while you toil to win the bread,
  Due strength the wine imparts.

By mutual labours, mine and thine,
  A household bread we eat;
And inward tenderness and joy
  Are still a cordial sweet.

Oh! care with comfort will combine
  For those the happiest wed;
But if we never want for wine
  We'll never fail of bread.

MARRIAGE.

The dawn of love in the heart is as the
" morning darkness spread upon the mountains "
to some dweller on level lands, who, awaking,
finds himself in the hill country: momently the

sun brightens, and the shadowy mysteries of the mountains disclose their wonders. Marriage is a deep-rooted tree. Strong may it be as a cedar, fruitful as a vine, having great boughs, and abundant in blossoms. Home is the tent we pitch beneath the wide shadow, and in which we receive visits from the angels at the cool and quiet evening. Evermore "a new song" sounds over the world from the birds that sing among the branches of this firm-rooted tree. And though strong winds blow often against it, bringing with them deluging rains of grief, it does but root itself more firmly, and presently there is around it an air sweet and still, and above it a serene, unclouded heaven. And even as the outmost fibres of a great tree's roots extend beyond the tips of its far-spreading branches, so for new experiences of life new and far-extending roots of love are ready ; and, wide as may be the expanse of bough and foliage, the tree is upborne and nourished. And though sense be the ground in which the marriage-tree is planted, it is as the earth, over which grass and flowerage, nourished by the purest dews of heaven, spread themselves—an earth we tread upon, yet honour. Whenever in our life the spiritual and the sensuous are at one, sense is no longer as a dark, dangerous storm-cloud, or as a heavy, blighting fog upon the marshes; but is as water dispersed in air, which makes the blue of heaven more soft and deep; and as dark earthy fuel kindled, which is unseen because of the bright, pure fires that it sustains.   The youth before he loves is as a vessel formed for the water, but as yet moored to the land. In movement alone upon waves that rise and fall can the graces of its outline, the power and beauty of its spars and sails, be manifested.   The love of woman becomes to him as a sea open to heaven, whose bosom, yielding to the vessel of his life, sustains it, and mirrors clearly its form and movements. As for woman, before she loves her heart is a garden of the north, rich and productive; but love changes it into a garden of the south, richer, fuller of beauty, fragrance, and luxuriance. If woman is the " glory of man," she is also a ray from the glory of God, who, in replenishing the earth with maidens, wives, and mothers, ever newly embodies for us ideas of delight, that rest everlastingly in the stillness of his pure unfathomed spirit. Man is known by his thoughts and devisings, and so is the Maker of men. Womanhood and infancy are revelations of the heart of God. He then that would

increase knowledge of his God—let him consider
his mother or his child—let him look in the eyes
of his wife, the beauty of which may have
perhaps been ripening for him through a long
summer of affection ; or if his soul is now, after
weakness, strengthened with a true love, and
God has thus clothed his spirit with light, and
girded him with gladness, perhaps now first
painting a rainbow upon the dark clouds of his
fortune, then let him, as he contemplates the
woman of his hope, adore the Giver of good gifts,
who lives and loves for ever.   The heart of both
the youth and the maiden is, with its many free
and blossoming affections, like a cluster of fair,
sweet-scented flowers.   Some flowers fall, but
some remain, and love is the setting of the fruit.
And as oft-times many germs unite to form a
single fruit, so love absorbs into itself the various
yearnings and affections of the soul, which lose
therein their separateness, but not their virtues.
Imparting these, they make love to grow to a
nutritious largeness; and as it ripens, marriage
becomes to it a strong defensive covering.   The
love of God, the "primal love," is as the pure
white light, which is one, yet has in it manifold-
ness of adorning power.   Sexal love is as a rainbow, in which are the elemental loves united, yet

inseparable. Of God is the beginning and the
continuance of love; the day-spring and the
day-course of this wonderful "Lord and Giver
of life." Fair colourings, and ravishing odorous
winds of the morning, must pass, but the orb of
the day remains in his power. Of God is the
sufficing grace and comeliness of the maiden—
of Him the high hope and purpose of the youth.
But of Him also the carefulness of wife and
husband; the beauty and security, the discipline
and the sorrows, of home. He makes families
like a flock, and watcheth over them as a shepherd, a "chief shepherd." He scatters young
children as the morning dewdrops, very plentifully. For these His hand has formed the breasts
of the mother; His Spirit devised their satisfying
richness. He has said to man and to woman,
Be ye to each other solace and strength, as
wayfarers together on the difficult road of life.
And He, coming to the home, can make the
long-wedded say, late in their feast of marriage
life, Surely the good wine has been kept till
now.

Adjoining the above, Theophilus has written—Infancy is lovable notwithstanding fret-
fulness and the whooping-cough. And the idea
of marriage is inspiringly sacred, notwithstanding

the farce, and vulgarity, and woe, and crime,
that the strange story of sexal behavings and
experiences reveals to us. The need of a seventh
commandment, and of the lighter and graver
admonitions of prudence and spiritual wisdom
respectively, shall not make me forget the original designation of woman, "a help meet for
man," nor cease to be an earnest believer, "that
he that getteth a wife getteth a good thing;"
that is, at least, if his wife be more than a *thing*.
She must have a true and tender womanly
heart. A "fine lady" is but a painted sepulchre
for a man to bury his dead happiness in.

Here is Trinal's account of

THE NEW WIFE'S INTRODUCTION TO THE OLD STUDY.

Come hither with me, lady dear,
　Love, come and see;
Alone you cannot enter here,
　For I have got the key.
Now, if you ever want, my love,
　Any thing with me,
Hither you must gently come
　To know if I am free:
Busy indeed must be the hour
　I cannot rise for thee.

This is my study, lady dear,
   Its uses are most plain,
The night has often found me here,
   My zeal could not refrain;
So hours of darkness I have pass'd
   In all a student's pain.
Most studiously studying
   The way your love to gain;
And well you know, my darling one,
   I laboured not in vain.

A man of letters, lady dear,
   I am, you are aware;
And this a packet is, of yours,
   Close fastened up with care;
Of different sizes, like the stars,
   That make the evening fair;
Love in the writing peeps and hides,
   Like stars in twilight air;
So modest my sweet star of life,
   Sweet fixèd star you were.

These are the poets, lady dear,
   And that an old divine,'
And yonder ragged-coated books
   Are full of wisdom fine;
And well you know these volumes bright
   That in their binding shine—
Beauty without and truth within,
   Fitly they combine;
You gave them, love, and like thyself
   Should be a gift of thine.

Upon this sofa, lady dear,
  I often used to lie ;
Watching intent the quiet moon,
  Slow pacing in the sky;
And still her beauty seem'd like yours,
  For grace and dignity;
And looking long, this thought would bring
  A tear into my eye;
What were the earth without the moon?
  Without you what were I ?

Books are my flowers, lady dear;
  That open one you see,
Is one at which I am at work
  As earnest as a bee;
My study is my garden, love,
  A place of toil for me,
But many of the flowers sweet
  Will give delight to thee;
So as a sipping butterfly,
  Most welcome shall you be.

Your household wisdom, lady dear,
  I value not the less,
That you a heart and intellect
  Cultured well possess;
So all the woman in the wife
  Unites my home to bless.
Sweet are thy face and form, and sweet
  Thy conjugal caress;
And sweet thy piety and sense,
  And sweet thy gentleness.

Here much and often, lady dear,
  I hope to work for you;
And for my God, and for the world,
  In careful studies true.
And you shall ever help me, love,
  To keep the right in view,
And ever to my growing thought
  Your word shall be as dew:
And he who join'd us heart and hand
  Will bless as hitherto.

SENTIMENT.

Bulbs will grow for a single season in water, but they will not flower or grow healthily the next season, unless they be put in earth; so it is with our minds. They will blossom in seclusion nourished by thought; but the season of blossom passed, their vitality must be renewed by the work and experience of life, which is as the earth to them. From dark, rough, common life, stony and earthy, springs beauty and vigour. Yet the plant, though removed from the water, must be watered; must have influence of sentiment, of imaginative thought. Wholesome sentiment is rain, which makes the fields of daily life fresh and odorous. We often speak contemptuously of the sentimentalist, and we do so because his feeling is not real; or, if real, has no proportionateness to a right activity. He is tawdry, or conceited, or designing. Truly fine natures dislike finery, but coarse ones may dislike both fineness and finery. There are some who have no more heart for fine thoughts than they have ear for fine music. But fine thoughts are to pure and deep feeling what fine growths are to a warm, summery climate. Flowers and trees grow in the earth, and thoughts noble and fine, flowers of a transient goodliness, and cedars of stately, euduring growth, are rooted in and have sustenance from reality. We may good-humouredly laugh at or indignantly expose the dressy, foppish, hypocritical exhibitors of prettinesses and tendernesses, and yet earnestly affirm that the imaginative thinker, the poet and the artist, are most practical men; quite as practical as the butcher and the baker. The thinker and the poet must be students and lovers of the world. They may or may not know a little of engineering and the funds, but they must know much of human character and experiences. Their practicalness is shown in the bestowal of joys, and hopes, and faith. Under their influence the world quickens and shapens.

In the world as it exists, there is ever a longing
to possess a pure and lofty idea of things, and
by this idea to produce changes—a new world.
This longing utters itself, and nurtures itself, by
the imaginative thinkers, whether they be poets
or prosists. True-hearted poesy becomes, as we
may say, the world's wife.   Here is an account
of the world's marriage: good came of it, though
many such marriages must there be before all
the New Truths and the New Things will be
born that mankind require:—

THE WORLD'S MARRIAGE.

The rough World, weary with his work,
　　One evening sat alone;
And said—Oh that I had a wife!
Purer then would be my life,
　　What follies have I done!
Stubborn and fierce, I'm full of sin,
Yet tenderness I feel within.

Sweet Poetry, love-worthiest maid,
　　Even then was wandering near,
And with her clear and silent eye
Fix'd on the clear and silent sky,
　　Watch'd for the earliest star;
And stood before the rough World's face
In majesty of bloom and grace.

Straight from his heart the morning broke,
   Spread on each cheek a flush;
And as she turning saw him stand
In bearded beauty close at hand,
   Love robed her in a blush;
She was the pale red moon at full,
   Fronting the bright sun powerful.

They wedded, and a son was born,
   His name they call'd—the New;
His earliest infancy was blest
With milk, and smiles, and bosom rest;
   And as the nursling grew,
Father and mother in the boy
Saw themselves, with wondering joy.

His young heart was a morning heaven,
   Broad, pure, and still;
Soon thoughts upbreathèd by desire,
Swelling, blending, mounting higher,
   Like clouds his spirit fill;
Dark-bright the towering masses range,
Boding showery wind and change.

The father frowns, the mother sweet
   Smiles upon her son;
'Mid freaks and waywardness of youth,
She marks his energy and truth;
   And for new follies done,
Wise and gentle, well she knows
Some plea of love to interpose.

The rough World, ever comforted
   And softened by his wife,
For her dear sake will much endure,
Himself he knows has not been pure,
   And equal in his life;
His strength, her spirit, he would see,
Her thought, his practicalness, she.

Thus waiting long, they watch and hope,
   The boy in power grows;
His streaming energy the while,
Still spreading like the waves of Nile,
   As widely overflows;
And not for spoil the waters rise,
Retiring, they shall fertilize.

" His blossoms first, now leaves he hath
   Needful, though not so fair."
Said Poetry, " So is our son
Like the almond and mezereon,
   And ripe fruits he will bear:
This middle leafy strength hath he,
That flower in fruit may perfect be."

The following lines are unexceptionably Pro-
testant. For did not an angel say, " Blessed art

thou among women," and Scripture record the
words?

ONE GREAT AMONG THE MOTHERS.

We'll thank our God for every birth,
   And bless with love each mother pure;
Rejoicing in the peopled earth,
   And Lives that ever may endure.

For one did nourish at her breast
   The world's Redeemer, meek and strong;
In her are all the mothers blest
   Since He so blest the babes among.

The dewy lilies opening shine
   With the fresh morning sweet above;
So shone the baby face divine
   Turned mother-wards for beams of love.

The world's great Friend then loved but one,
   With thoughts of Him her heart was stored;
Soon as her joy her griefs begun,
   Oh, honour her, while He's adored!

For sweeter than the spikenard given
   By her whose love all earth shall hear,
That love which nursed the Child from Heaven,
   With sanctity of hope and fear.

P

When veiling darkness is withdrawn
   That Day may break the powers of Night;
How beautiful the lowly dawn,
   Whence issues forth the Sun in might!

Mother of Christ! so lovely thou
   Hast to the generations been;
And, Sister, we will love thee now,
   Pure Sister, of deep heart serene.

CHAPTER XI.

REST.

The day is over,
    The feverish, careful day:
Can I recover
    Strength that has ebbed away?
Can even sleep such freshness give,
That I again shall wish to live?

Let me lie down,
    No more I seek to have
A heavenly crown,
    Give me a quiet grave;
Release and not reward I ask,
Too hard for me life's heavy task.

Now let me rest,
    Hushed be my striving brain,
My beating breast;
    Let me put off my pain,
And feel me sinking, sinking deep
Into an abyss of sleep.

The morrow's noise,
   Its anguish hope and fear,
Its empty joys,
   Of these I shall not hear;
Call me no more, I cannot come;
I'm gone to be at rest, at home.

Earth undesired,
   And not for heaven meet;
For one so tired
   What's left but slumber sweet,
Beneath a grassy mound of trees,
Or at the bottom of the seas?

Yet let me have,
   Once in a thousand years,
Thoughts in my grave,
   To know how free from fears
I sleep, and that I there shall lie
Through undisturbed eternity.

And when I wake,
   Then let me hear above
The birds that make
   Songs not of human love:
Or muffled tones my ears may reach
Of storms that sound from beach to beach.

But hark! what word
   Breathes through this twilight dim?

" Rest in the Lord,
    Wait patiently for Him;
Return, O soul, and thou shalt have
A better rest than in thy grave."

My God, I come;
    But I was sorely shaken:
Art thou my home?
    I thought I was forsaken:
I know Thou art a sweeter rest
Than earth's soft side or ocean's breast.

Yet this my cry!—
    " I ask no more for heaven,
Now let me die,
    For I have vainly striven."
I had, but for that word from Thee,
Renounced my immortality.

Now I return;
    Return, O Lord, to me:
I cannot earn
    That Heaven I'll ask of Thee;
But with Thy Peace amid the strife,
I still can live in hope of Life.

The careful day,
    The feverish day is over;
Strength ebbed away,
    I lie down to recover;
With sleep from Him I shall be blest,
Whose word has brought my sorrows rest.

We have entered Chapter XI. of our book,
and have given but little biographic detail.   It
was not our purpose to show of Theophilus how
he was born, cradled, schooled, tail-coated, col-
leged, and the like.   Some of the gums and the
fruits of his tree of being, with also sprigs and
blossoms, we have given—not a picture of the
tree and a history of its growth.   Here, however,
is an autobiographic word.   "My life for many
years was like a running fight on the sea-shore,
such as I have read of in campaigns—on one
side the great sea of the eternal, sometimes all
terrible roar and cloud, and sometimes broad
peace and deep inexpressible hope; on the other
side, the frowning unscalable rocks of worldly
custom, prejudice, and fact.   Sick in body and
heart, I was harassed from the rear and from
among the rocks as I advanced, by questions,
doubts, dismays, pains, errors, longings, and
accusings."   This is not very definite, though
significant.   We believe the truth is, that Trinal
was naturally a frail-bodied man, with yet a
vigorous, endeavouring kind of constitution; that
in him were singularly blended active and contemplative tendencies; that religious thirstings
and strivings were necessities of his being; and
that for long years he endured still renewing

physical and spiritual sufferings. His mother purposed he should be a preacher, and his own heart purposed it too. But he found, to his great sadness—and, foolish man! to his surprise at the first—that among the loves that do not run smoothly, is the love of witnessing for what you believe is Divine Truth. His first preachings were in retired places, where the hearts of many hearers being needy and devout, they said plainly of his words—They are good. Preaching afterwards in places where there were more of those persons whom he used to call " frivolous Evangelicals," it was agreed that his visage and form were ghostly, which at that time was quite true; that his manner was abominably nervous, which was then partly true; and that his words, whatever else they might be, certainly were not "the Gospel," which Trinal affirms was never true at all. Fire there was in him, none denied—but it was strange fire. Some said there was light too—others, that it was all darkness to them—and others again, that there was light to be sure, but it burst on you and blinded you. So, with little opportunity of becoming known any where, where he was known he was by few judged favourably. In one of his memorandum books he says, "I suffered much misery, from which a strong man with a mind, a heart, and a hand, might have saved me." With one or more persons whom he thought might prove such, he seems to have formed slight acquaintance. He was a ship in distress, and they ships of deliverance that hove in sight. And he made his signals of distress; but surely these must have been mistaken, for, says he, " I have seen a ship of hope make sail away from me as from a privateer, which I suppose I was thought." However, in these dark days he had some times of refreshing: "And little things," he writes, "in the time of a great and very private distress, have surprising comfort in them." A rationally Evangelical "minister" who had never seen him, hearing of him, thought good to ask him to preach. He did so. And the kindly trust thus shown him was graven on his heart as with a pen of iron on the rock. Here is a little poem of his which may or may not refer to his work of ministering, but at least is applicable:—

PURPOSE.

I had an out-blown crocus, and as yet but one,
It opened early when the sun first shone ;
But a hailstone smote it, and its life is done.

I had an uttered thought, my cherished one,
I spread it out freely, dewed with joy begun;
But cold words bowed it, and my hope was gone.

Yet it folded to re-open, for with life is power:
The crocus it was severed from the stalk that bore;
But my heart still bears my thought, and I can hope
once more.

———◆———

Nor do we think it will displease any Evangelical man, unless he be of the "frivolous" sort, if we give the following paper, which represents a time of delirium. Not all were Israelites indeed that were of Israel's race, so not all are Christian that are of the Christian Churches. As Christ addressed Jews, so must we sometimes speak to Christians.—Ye say that He is your God, yet you have not known Him; ye say that He is your Saviour, yet you have not known Him; ye say that Christianity is your religion, yet you have not known it. "Christian" is and shall remain a most honourable title, yet have there been times and places in which, with sorrowful emphasis, it might be asked, "What can be more opposite than Christ and a Christian, if such as these be Christians?"

Grace in this paper is Trinal's mother; it was one of his names for her.

Theop. Don't let those bad people come near me—those Christians.

Grace. Why, you are a Christian yourself, Theophilus !

Theop. I ? What ! I ? Take them away. They look like black goats butting at me. Let somebody stand near me that loves me.

Grace. I am with you, dearest—I am here.

Theop. A little water, if you please—a little water.—What time is it ?

Grace. Take a little of this—here is some orange.

Theop. What time is it? what time ?—Oh, it is very hot !—where is my mother ?

Grace. Here—with you. It is I who am giving you the orange.

Theop. Is it morning? I wish it was morning !—There are no birds in August !

Grace. Birds, Theophilus ?

Theop. I went through the wood in the afternoon, and there were no birds. In the spring, every tree had a bird. I went to make my sermon. It was very silent, but it was sultry.—Oh, my head !—it is heavy and hot like the wood—but no birds. I feel very full of things; but it is so dark. But never mind, Theophilus—never mind.

Grace. Dear one, I cannot bear to hear those tones.

Theop. Tones! My tones are not harsh. Who says so? I know that I love to speak the truth: who is it that does not like to hear me? Why not?

Grace. Theophilus, morning is coming now. I'll hold back the curtain. Look!

Theop. Death is cold——

Grace. There is One who gives life, and who keepeth alive:—we will trust in Him. Do not speak of death, dearest!

Theop.—

> Death is cold; but so is dawn
> When the faint pale face of morn,
> Skyward turn'd with closèd eyes,
> In life-awaiting slumber lies——

Grace. You must sleep now a little, Theophilus;—try.

Theop. I had a dream.—There was a deep place like a well. I bent over it with a torch, to look if there was water; but the torch went out. Then I lighted another; and it fell in, and I fell in too. So I knew that there was water, for I felt it. It was very deep, and I was stunned and nearly drowned. But I found myself at the top of the well again, I do not know how. And I gave people the water; and some drank, and thanked me; but many laughed at me, and would not take any, but threw stones at me.—I wish I could sleep.

Grace. You must try. I shall sit by you You are more composed now.

Theop. My head will not stop; it keeps moving round like a windmill. Do the trees move? Is there a wind? I wish there was some wind. Make me a wind, mother.

Grace. I will fan you a little.

Theop. That is good. Oh, that is very good! —Did not I say something about Christians just now? Do not let any body be near me but you. —A little more of that cool, gentle air, please.

[*She fans him; he sleeps.*

When the soul is dim, the man is dark. Only by fulness of life comes fulness of light. We cannot have fulness of life, but we may have reality and increase. It is the "eternal life" that becomes Light. Only as we partake of it can we learn of event and behaviour, of self and of humanity. When he who holds place as teacher has not Life, he has not Light. Then he becomes as

THE DARK DOCTOR.

With sad appropriateness termed D.D.,
Some may like Dr. Dimsoul Darkman be :
So learned he can quite dispense
With vision and intelligence.
He hath a creed, he hath a tongue,
He had a heart when he was young ;
But—very melancholy fact !—
'Tis like a bell that time hath crackt !
Which by this certain mark is known—
His speech is clatter without tone.
His creed is sound as any post,
A growth which former life has lost ;
And though his manner polished be
As shiny, new mahogany,
His sermons one another follow
Like echoes in a cavern hollow.
The truth from him is mouldy crust,
His word a wind with blinding dust ;
And in his fog of speech you fumble
Till at the plainest things you stumble.
His character may thus be told :
Nor good nor bad, nor hot nor cold ;
Spotless, perhaps, as downy goose,
But to the world as little use.

Like wind from an old tomb,
　On a chilly winter's day,
Where bones of generations
　Are mouldering away ;

Is the voice of Dr. Darkman,
　Cold and dull,
And the body of his doctrine
　No soul makes beautiful.

He and his people
　Are a corpse stiff and stark,
Silently decaying
　In its death-chamber dark.
And to veil the ghastliness
　From head to feet,
Exterior decency
　Is the woven white sheet.

Oh! Dr. Dimsoul,
　Reason try and Love;
Remember thou art earthly—
　There is one God above:
In his pity he hath given us
　His well-beloved Son;
With whose Word and whose sorrows
　You may thrill each one.

Religion is as ointment,
　· Most choice, most pure;
Of costliness and fragance,
　For comfort and for cure;
But dead flies are in it—
　The dead creeds are they—
They give to it their savour,
　Take its own away.

The heavens most ancient
　No new God declare :
Though a changing astronomy
　Beams on each star :
And in love-bright glory
　Still the Christ hath sway ;
He, the Truth, is eternal,
　Creeds for a day.

Each new time its new thought
　Must in new words tell ;
And the old primary heart tones
　In new music swell ;
And in grander theologies,
　Higher truth be shown ;
But unchanged 'mid all changes,
　God's heart and our own.

Words of warmth and brightness
　We in vain desire ;
Ye give us dull words—the ashes
　Of a nigh-quenched fire.
Oh ! the mouth-man and the heart-man
　Different they be,
As death and life, light and dark,
　Ice and charity !

The great human heart
　Is a world-covering vine ;
And ever in new seasons
　The new clusters shine :

> But ye feed us with the raisins
>   Of another century's sun,
> Whilst around hang in sweetness
>   The grapes of our own.

"It is still true," said Theophilus to his mother, as they sat one evening watching the sunset, "that 'the hungry sheep look up, and are not fed.' Poor sheep! Though they neither relish the taste of what is given them, nor find it nourishing, yet some of them seem sorrowfully and in simplicity to believe, that there is no hay sweeter and no grass greener. And then human sheep cannot be always eating, even when the food is of the best. They need to repose in the pleasant pastures, and to listen to the streams as they flow. This is forgotten. Bread is a good thing, but so are sunshine and rest good things. Our people should not alone be as the hungry seated at a feast, but as work-people come out of busy cities into the broad, clean country, and this on a fine summer's day. The churches where they gather should be as hills of Zion, on which resting, they may enjoy the beautiful prospects that lie around, wonder at the works of God, and by their gladness of heart learn to love Him better."

SATURDAY EVE.

As mother stoops to kiss her child
  Before she takes the light away,
And leaves him to his rest : so mild
The heaven over earth is bending,
  So lovingly withdraws the day.

' Tis Saturday's dusk that darkens now,
  How calmly kind the heaven is !
So mother a more serious brow,
Assumes because the week is ending,
  And gives her child a tenderer kiss.

HYMN FOR SUNDAY.

The Lord is rich and merciful !
  The Lord is very kind !
Oh ! come to Him, come now to Him,
  With a believing mind.
His comforts they shall strengthen thee,
  Like flowing waters cool ;
And He shall for Thy spirit be
  A fountain ever full.

The Lord is glorious and strong,
  Our God is very high ;
Oh ! trust in Him, trust now in Him,
  And have security.

Q

He shall be to thee like the sea,
  And thou shalt surely feel
His wind, that bloweth healthily
  Thy sicknesses to heal.

The Lord is wonderful and wise,
  As all the ages tell :
Oh ! learn of Him, learn now of Him,
  Then with thee it is well.
And with his light thou shalt be blest,
  Therein to work and live ;
And He shall be to thee a rest
  When evening hours arrive.

———————

" To-night I sat an hour at the western window—my prospect over corn-fields and woods to
a broken range of hills beyond.   I watched the
grand and comforting sunset, and enjoyed, as I
could not but phrase it to myself, 'the music of
the stillness.'   Then I fell into thoughts of death
as the great consecrator.   When our friend is
gone, his last days spread a mellow brightness
over his life—it becomes a country covered with
the evening sunshine.   The death on the cross
was an awful sunset—the great light of the
world went down amidst dark clouds, which it
touched with fiery grandeur.   And now the
whole earthly life of the Redeemer is a rich land

of fields and hills, overspread with a light, full,
still, and soft. In such a light waves for the generations the gospel bread-corn, ever newly sown
for new harvests; and on the great mountains
of thought there abides a deep and solemn
flush."

"Surely some who teach from the pulpit might
be much benefited by a discreet use of the magic
lantern. There might be a slide for each pew,
or at least a goodly number of slides, representing old and young, healthy and sick, people
at their trades and in their homes, groups of
men and women, with diversity of expression
and costume. Surely if such a phantasmagoria
passed before ministers on the walls of their
studies, their preaching would have more soul
and sense in it. Sinners, like men, are of divers
sorts, and have divers histories. As plants may
alike droop from different causes, so men may
be alike hurt and endangered by different sins.
In one plant, an insect small but strong may
consume the buds, so that they sicken and fall.
A great loathsome slug may slowly fatten itself
upon the juices of another. Another has no
soil, hence no roots, and seems the mockery of
what we know it might be; and yet another is
under the dark, close shade of a wall or tree: it

has neither light nor air, and its every leaf shows
diseased feebleness. The like evils, and many
more, are among men. The budding promise of
one man's nature seems always to fall; some
sin, not perhaps obvious, or of mark and note,
consumes it. Offensive, slimy indolence kills or
grievously hurts another. Another is all frivo-
lity; his heart has never been ploughed up, and
the surface soil is thin: he is a lean, stunted
soul. And so yet another lives under the influence of some evil fashion or evil person; and,
if not saved from the blight and gloom of this
wall or tree, he must wither away. Remember
the sinner in the man, but remember also the
man in the sinner. The merchants, the labourers,
the princes, the philosophers, are sinful souls;
but the sinners in their various kinds are variously partakers of humanity, and its labour and
sorrow."

Here is a peep at one sort of Saturday night—
that of an over-worked, scanty-pursed man. He
has come home now to his careful wife, and she
has wept a tear or two for him and for their
troubles; and now he is comforting her:—

SATURDAY NIGHT.

Come, cheer your heart and clear your eyes,
Look into the flowers, look up to the skies;
There is love in the God of mysteries.

Body and brain, I am weary quite;
As the clock must tick, so I must write—
Wound up in the morning to go till night.

But smiles and hopes should shine through woe,
For green leaves peep even through the snow;—
Remember, my love, you told me so.

God knows the events of our hidden lives,
And to temper sorrows comfort gives.
If William is weak, yet Mary thrives.

Thanks, love, for those tears, though I wished them
    gone,
They were shed for my pain that you make your
    own;
Now, smile me a rainbow, your heart the sun.

True treasure for me is this face of thine;
Shall I fret for a house that is large and fine,
With furniture gay, and pictures, and wine?

Far better be poor, than a heart to own
Like a sour small cherry, mostly stone;
Being rich, but rich for one's self alone.

Yet money is good : it is bread for life,
It nurtures the babes, it comforts the wife,
Brings plenty and rest for want and strife.

Earned shillings are sweet as drops of rain ;
And sad hearts, bowed with care and pain,
Bedewed with money, grow bright again.

A time shall come—is it near at hand ?—
When the heart and head shall for good command
The gathered wealth of the labouring hand.

When who so will work may hope and enjoy,
When man shall man as his brother employ,
And love shall the gold-glutton wholly destroy.

Meanwhile the world, that grinds on and on,
Like a barrel-organ, its Mammon tune,
Now ceases a little—the week is done.

And, my love, my wife, if the morrow be fair,
We will see the fresh fields, will breathe fresh air,
Be with God in His house, and every where.

CHAPTER XII.

THE BIBLE: A DIALOGUE.

Man. What art thou, Bible? Art thou not the great crumbling yew that still grows in the burial-place of the earth's ancestry? Thy roots are by father Adam's head, and under thy shade the elders of the world rest. Thy branches are still gravely green, but thy decay is advanced and advancing. Is it not so?

Bible. I am both antiquity and eternity.

M. Eternity abides, but antiquity must perish.

B. Must antiquity perish? Dost thou not mark in the sand-stone the traces of the rain-drop that fell ten thousand years ago? Dost thou not consider with rejoicing admiration the skeletons of old leviathans that swam in the earth's early oceans? Art thou not ever learning by that which was, and is not, and yet is? Small things of the old time are now big to thee with import and with interest. The light of thy studies grows to thee as the light of a rounding moon. And the mild and thoughtful glow reflects to thee the beam of a sun that shone on times and scenes that have died only for themselves, but rise again to live for thee. The Lord give thee understanding, thou that speak not lightly of antiquity perishing.

M. Thou sayest, Bible, that thou art eternity.

B. He that knoweth and honoureth me, knoweth and honoureth the eternal. Thou, O man, art mortal, and shalt, if thou be faithful, put on immortality. I am immortal, and shall put off mortality. My oft-unfolded pages shal be at last folded as a vesture. But my word is the same, and it shall not fail. The earth is a temple, and I am the altar; from me streams heavenwards the ever-burning fire. But, when He shall come with light and with fire whose right it is to reign, he shall take me into himself, and I shall be known in him as he has been known in me.

M. Speak yet of thyself, Bible; for who can speak as thou? Tell me what thou art.

B. I will speak to thee in emblem. It is my manner. The bride hath her attire and her ornament, and the prophet his parable. He may no more speak without beauty than without truth. Aaron's pure linen is fine linen. His vestments are for holiness, and for glory, and for beauty.

M. I honour thee, and will hearken ; speak of thyself as it pleaseth thee.

B. I am a map, on which the eyes of generations have pondered. The venerable charter of your highest liberties. I am as an old cathedral, solemn and vast, around whose circuit and among whose windings eternity whispers in the stillness, as the voice of ocean in its shells· Upon the stones have your fathers' feet rested, and from them have their voices risen. I am as Petra the city of tombs, tombs in the rock. Therein lie the great ones of the old days, each in his house ; Judaism rests in its sculptured sepulchre, and the prophets of God are embalmed imperishably. I am as the massive head of an Egyptian Memnon. The sands of centuries drift over me ; the wind again scatters them, and my rest is immovable. Colossal and majestic, undreadingly I confront all storms, and with sorrowful but hopeful eyes gaze fixedly upon the wastes of time. I am an ancient forest; in me are trees of all kinds. Some stand fair in their beauty and proportion ; others are gnarled, and of a rough strength. You walk through me in a light dusky but solemn, and, ever and anon, you break from thickest gloom, and the clear heaven shines openly above you. You tread on herbs of healing, and plants of rarest beauty; and as you look around, your eye is ever catching some flower now conspicuous, but hitherto unseen. I am like a cavern—dark, but full of gems. I send forth the sound of many waters that flow from unseen depths, pure and refreshing. Your eye may not penetrate. The vastness awes you. You tremble, but rejoice. I am as the wonderful but changing firmament, which sometimes is a sky of storms, wherein are clouds dark as night or of a lurid brightness, shadowing the soul with awe; and sometimes an open sapphire vault, a blue heaven, pure and deep as the thoughts of God, in which refreshing airs wander like spirits, even the spirits his messengers; but the great sun dwells there, giving life when visible, and sustaining it when unseen. And even as the natural sun bends worlds around it in harmonious movement, whilst it creates and conserves life and fertility in their different parts, and brings forth an infinitely varied beauty: so the great Sun-Truth of—God manifest in humanity, gives movement and harmony to the whole system of truths; life, force, and pro-

ductiveness to each, even the least several portion, and, by its illuminating beam, enables us
to view all iu a completeness impressive and
majestic.

M. Bible, I will worship thee.

B. See thou do it not. I am a servant, as
thou. I am but of thy brethren the prophets.
Worship Him who is the Light of lights.

M. Art thou not at the least a king?

B, I am a king, though I be but a servant.
"I am understanding; I have strength." And
he that hath most strength by fullest understanding of my wisdom, shall be a prince in that
great company of souls that wait for, and shall
welcome and inaugurate, the reign of Him who
cometh to rule and to be loved as the true and
only everlasting King.

M. Bible, what shall I do?

B. Flatter me not; follow me. Say not,
"This is the temple of God: see what stones
and buildings are here," when thou dost not
worship, but defilest my sanctity with thy foolish,
thy earthy, thy selfish mind. Count me as a
friend whose greeting is generous, and whose
heart is large; but know that I will rebuke thee
sharply for all that is false and mean. Come
thou in naked sincerity, and bathe in my cleans-

ing rivers. Come thou whenever it is morning with thee; when the earliest beam of hope and of thought strikes. Come, drink of the flowing brook of my counsel, and, as thou drinkest, lift up the head, pray, and give thanks.

M. Bible, I will be a trumpet to sound thy praise. With what certain and simple sound may I proclaim thee?

B. Proclaim me the firmament in which He shines who is the light of the world. Only a sun can be a lamp to suffice a world: only God a Saviour to suffice mankind. Believest thou in Christ the Saviour?

M. Alas! Bible, I believe in sorrow.

B. But believest thou in sin? There be more that wear crape for their sorrows, than sackcloth for their sins. If thou servest the Evil World, at the last Evil shall say to thee of thy sorrows, "What are these to me? see thou to these: fool, to complain—too late, too late!" But if thou servest the True One—the Saviour, he shall say to thee of thy sorrows, " What are these to thee? I bear them: I change them. By mine own sorrows and victory have I resolved them into joys." Sin without a Saviour is the black cloud of a storm advancing; but sin to him that believeth in Christ is the black cloud of a storm retiring.

M. Bible, I believe; still help thou mine unbelief. This Saviour shall be my Saviour for
ever and ever. He will be my guide even unto
death. I rejoice, and yet I fear.

B. The lightning glared on thee as thou didst
journey a dangerous path. It showed thee an
abyss at thy foot. But hadst thou not seen,
thou couldst not have been saved. The abyss,
not the sight of it, was thy peril. The sight of
the evil was the occasion of thy terror, but the
condition of thy deliverance. And if thou sawest
an abyss below, thou sawest also the countenance
and hand of a friend above thee. But the sudden
light passed, and it fell dark again—and so thou
again fearedst. And often thou wilt see thy
Saviour by the transitory flash of a bright summer
lightning, rather than by the steady shining of a
bright summer day. But call, in the dark, on a
Saviour whom thou seest not, and he will answer
thee; he will come to thee, and hold thee by the
hand while shadows remain : and soon the morning shall dawn, and he be with thee, thy counsellor,
master, and companion.

M. Bible, thou comfortest me. I will sing.

B. Sing, but fight too. Let the song of faith
spirit thee for the fight of faith. Art thou assured
of a Saviour's strength and presence? sing thank-

fully.   But be thou also strong to overcome as he overcame.   Praise God by the harmony and power of thy life, as well as by the melody of thy thanksgiving.   If thou goest to God at last as one that hath fought the fight, hath kept the faith, and hath overcome—thou mayest also depart, as thou art told the old lark doth.   He collects his strength for one last flight and one last song, strikes upwards to the " serenest heights" of heaven, and breathing his soul out in praise, in the midst of his melody he droops his wing, and falls dead upon the green earth he has so often charmed and cheered.

M. Bible, I bless thee, and I bless thy glory and thy beauty.

B. Which is the greater, the golden candle-stick or the lights it bears?   My books are the many-branched golden candlestick—my " word of life" is the yet more golden light thereon, the light which goeth not out at all.   Blessest thou my beauty?   Yea, and it shall be blessed.   But rather bless my truth, which beauty serves as a robe, a diadem, a pavilion.   Bless the light of my lights, and the glory of my beauties.   Bless your Lord and your God.

REASONING WITH GOD.

O hidden Lord, most wise and rich,
 Whom oft I love, but often fear;
Of light and dark, oft doubting which,
 Doth most upon Thy works appear:
Why, if in Thee no darkness is,
 So deep a shade on human kind?
If Thon be Father, tell me this,
 Why the sad heart, the troubled mind?

Then said a voice, "This truth within thee store,
And wait, believing, ere thou askest more:
Earth is a cloud which Time shall puff away,
Then shalt thou see the heaven and feel the day."

WISH AND RESPONSE.

The Heart said, Oh that thou wouldst hide me in the grave! The Truth said, He that endureth to the end shall be saved.

THE WISH.

He hath lain down to rest
 In the churchyard old;
He fears not the morrow,
 He feels not the cold.

At morning and at midnight
 And at evening chill,
The clock strikes loud,
 But he sleeps on still.

Hour passes hour,
 Yet he stirs not a limb:
The chimes in the tower
 Call in vain to him.

He will not turn and listen
 To the thunder in the sky;
At his little children's voices
 Will not start nor sigh.

Not once his head he raises,
 He will never know
Whether over him are daisies
 Or over him is snow.

He is hidden from calamities,
 Free from care and labour:
Oh, how quiet and how safe he is!
 I wish I were his neighbour.

THE RESPONSE.

But if thou art a Christian,
 why fearest thou the morrow?
And if thou art a soldier,
 why shrinkest thou from cold?
Bright as morning after rain
 shall thy heart be after sorrow;
And at solitary midnight
 thy song shall make thee bold.

And if thou art a workman,
    oh, listen to the hour
As it strikes for thee in tones that break
    and tremble in the wind ;
Like a voice of love still crying
    with tenderness and power,—
" Be thou neither of presuming
    nor despairing mind."

Wouldst thou wrap thee in thy dulness,
    and lie thee down and sleep,
When the chime of truths and mercies
    ever calls to worship new ;
Or, so long and so strong,
    and of such an ample sweep,
Strange event affrights thy country
    like a thunder rolling through ?

Dost thou ask for day a lighter load,
    for night a softer rest,
Wish that smiles were meat for children,
    and kisses could be bread ;
Say, Oh that man might build a home
    as bird provides a nest,
And that touch of loving hand
    could heal an aching head ?

Oh, traveller, still travel on,
    though sore of foot and slow ;
Let thy burden and thy company
    make heart and shoulder strong ;

R

Thou art guide to those thou lovest,
    through the summer and the snow,
And art carrying the gold
    for thy heavenly harp of song,

Thou'lt be neighbour to the dead
    when thou fallest in the fight;
Now thou'rt neighbour to the living,
    who would help and counsel borrow
And even till the chimes of heaven
    call thee to the light,
A neighbour thou shalt find in Him
    who was the Man of Sorrow.

A CHURCH WITH BELLS.

"Bells," said a child, " I want to go,
  Sir, to a church with bells."
And whether high, or broad, or low,
  With hope my spirit swells,
When such a church as this I find,
  And hear the heavenly chime;
Oh, then I have a holy mind,
  Oh, then a happy time.
And though my hours are weak and sad,
  I feel my life sublime;
Of Love the first, and Love the last,
  If any service tells,
All my anxiety is past,
  I've found a church with bells.

I to an ancient abbey went,
   And sat beside a tomb ;
'Twas on a showery day in Lent,
   But near the Day of Bloom.
Along with me a blind man knelt,
   No glories could he see ;
But, oh ! the music how he felt—
   " Have mercy, Lord !" sang we ;
And angels from the window smiled
   Upon both him and me.
Said I, " Antiquity and grace
   Blend here their holy spells ;
In truth this is a noble place,
   This is a church with bells."

Whitewash'd, upon a windy hill,
   There stood a building square ;
I enter'd gently, hoping still
   That bells there might be there.
"Come, weary folks," an old man said,
   " You *have* come—come again,
'Tis every night you need your bed,
   Not only now and then.
Lord, give us better, safer rest."
   The people said, "Amen."
And when the kindly talk I heard,
   That angry sorrow quells,
" Here sounds," said I, " the inviting word,
   This is a church with bells."

I went the silent Friends to see,
   And there no bells could ring ;
For how can any music be
   Where nobody will sing ?
But as we all were sitting hush'd,
   Up rose a sister grey,
And said with face a little flush'd,
   " This is a sunny day,
And Jesus is our inward light
   To guide us on our way,"
" Ah, yes," said I, "this Sister pure
   The old glad tidings tells ;
And here, too, I am very sure
   I've found a church with bells."

Then by a door I heard men say,
   " He is not 'sound,' we fear,"
Thought I, before I turn away
   I'll try if bells are here.
" Quit you like men," a strong voice cried
   " Not hang the bulrush head ;
Our fathers' God is by our side,
   For truth our fathers bled.
Let no man sell his liberty,
   For butter or for bread."
Said I, " That's no unholy note,
   How loud and clear it swells ;
St. Paul's a stirring man to quote,—
   This, too's, a church with bells,"

Oh, I have got of sweet bells eight,
   And you may have the same ;
I ring them early, ring them late,
   And know them each by name :—,
There's Faith, and Hope, and Love, and Peace,
   And Joy, and Liberty,
And then, before the chime can cease,
   Patience and Victory ;
Come, neighbour, listen to the bells
   That ring for you and me.
When windy skies are all aflame,
   Of rest their chiming tells ;
We've never been since Jesus came,
   In want of Heavenly Bells.

THE MOUNTAIN CITY.

High o'er the mountains shines the Mount of Blessing,
   On which the Saviour hath His city builded ;
A highest height, high heaven itself caressing,
   Crown'd with bright clouds, with wealth of sunbeams
      gilded.
Beautiful refuge, hush'd in safe repose,
   Fountains of comfort still from thee are flowing ;
Within thee spring the heavenly lily and rose,
   Around, new corn, new grass are ever growing.

Ascend, ye Poor! still cries the King of nations,
   Rich in the bounty of unfailing pity ;
Your sighs and tears have been no vain oblations,
   Come, eat the fat things of the royal city.

For you the Kingdom-gate is ever open,
   The King's heart is the gate into His favour—
Humble beneath your burdens ye have spoken,
   Still rather of your love than of your labour.

Come up and rest, ye blessed of my Father,
   And with you bring the timid Mourners too;
Rouse them from grief with gentle words, for rather
   Will Mourners lie and weep, than to pursue
The comfort that they need, rise and begird
   Their failing loins with strength ; so help the faint,
Ye humble ones beloved, for God hath heard
   Your simple prayer and their sad complaint.

Come hither, too, ye Hungry and Athirst,
   Who love no husks nor the earth's meat of stone;
From the great deeps of righteousness there burst,
   Piercing as yet this happy hill alone,
The sweet, clear founts of truth, whose streams beside,
   The juicy bread-fruits of forgotten heaven,
Grow bounteously, their leaves no serpent hide,
   They flower anew for each day of the seven.

Ye Meek, come forward, ye who stand behind,
   This bread, this water, they are both for you;
Oh, be no longer of a doubting mind !
   Heavy the cross is, but the promise true.
Stronger is he who meekly bears his pain
   Than he who cleaves his foe and rules the earth;
The earth is yours, patience the fight shall gain,
   Sharp is the pain, but happy is the birth.

And with the meek, ye Merciful climb up,
   Mount to the light together, hand in hand;
Ye who have strew'd your corn and shared your cup,
   Look with your friends down on the widening land,
That yet shall be meek Mercy's favoured realm,
   Nourish'd by waters freely flowing hence;
No need of sword to smite, of shield and helm,
   For glorious peace shall be her own defence.

Far in the valleys, hidden from the noise
   Of crowds that lust and strive, your Lord descries
You, too, ye Pure in heart, and sends his joys
   Into the sorrow of your waiting eyes.
What look ye for, ye simple ones and sad?
   Why gaze ye still so earnestly above?
I hear your sudden song, your heart is glad,
   Far off ye see the City of His Love.

Yes, this is God, this long'd-for Light is He,
   And every beam is like his touch and kiss;
Come, from your valleys climb, the city see,
   And bring the Men of Peace to home and bliss.
Oft in the vale ye soothe their wounded heart,
   Then forth they go to quench the wanton fires,
Whose forky tongues strike with a serpent's dart,
   Whose grimy smoke infects the world's desires.

Ye children of the Highest, come, refresh
   Your torn and tired hearts in that true home,
Where spirit, loosed from the unpeaceful flesh,
   Rests on the sea of light, nor fears the foam

Of breakers that the dark and rocky world
  Throws off and up in restlesss fear and hate;
Towards, but not unto, this height are hnrl'd
  Passions, that with themselves, thcmselves must sate.

Oh, blest are ye who, Peaceful, Meek, and Pure,
  Yet calmly front the Persecutor's rage;
Brief is your rest, for ye must yet endure
  The world's attack, and all its might engage.
Descend anew, refresh'd with heavenly wine,
  Bear the great banner of God's righteousness;
Through His Son's heart, the holy gate Divine,
  He sends you forth to suffer and to bless.

For bless'd are ye, and therefore can ye bless,
  Lovers of good eternal, undefiled;
Be sure the opposing world ye shall possess,
  Though still by false and cruel tongues reviled.
Pierce ye the foe with salted words of fire,
  The pure, bright fire of love celestial,
And your reward shall be as your desire;
  With all the righteous prophets ye shall dwell.

Unscathed,though burnt; whole,although sawn asunder;
  Bright,though bemired; and powerful,though despised;
God's glory and his adversary's wonder,
  His love your own, that great reward ye prized.
Rejoice in hope, be glad exceedingly,
  Know ye not Him who builded hath this city?
Mighty the mount, but mightier far is He,
  His power is like His patience and His pity.

O'er the broad earth far shines the coming morning,
    Long hath the dawn upon this hill-top rested;
How long, O Lord, how long must still the scorning,
    The darkness with which earth is yet invested,
And quarrel of the wrestling winds endure,
    And hurtful fires from the confronting clouds?
Come from the city, come, with radiance pure,
    Descend the mountain, draw to Thee the crowds.

Bring the broad day: lo, leprous darkness kneeling,
    Says,"Lord,Thou wilt and Thou canst make me clean."
Earth's palsied servants all have need of healing;
    And our Proud Power knows that itself hath been
In office only for a heavenly king.
    Speak, and thy word shall every strength recruit,
Whose service fails us in the very thing,
    We hoped would yield us long-desired fruit.

Come, Lord, to Peter's house, our House of Faith,
    Where heavenly Love, mother of Charity,
By which Faith works his good, as Wisdom saith,
    Fever'd with weakness lies, ready to die;
Raise her—the whole earth needs her ministry;
    Thee first, and then her daughter, and her son
She will salute, and then look round and see
    What for us all may be most kindly done.

I wake!—what music wakes me from my vision?
    The joyful strain sinks to a wailing minor;
Must hope be still the common world's derision?
    No, hope returns, the song is louder, finer;

The major sank into the minor's sorrow,
   The minor rises to the major's glory;
So peace to-day changes to war to-morrow,
   Then triumph stands upon the field so gory.

Lord, does the way unto the Mount of Blisses,
   Not for a visit, but for lasting ease,
Lie across Calvary, where still there hisses
   The Serpent old, whose victim when he sees,
For him he weaves the folds of agony,
   Nor spares the Pure, the Peacemaker, the Meek,
The Merciful, the Poor,—so hungry he,—
   Upon the Just that mourn his hate to wreak?

E'en so, did not the Saviour speak the blessing,
   And then descend that He might bear the curse;
And then ascend once more, the throne possessing,
   To conquer which in pain he did immerse
His holy love, all the dark anguish bearing,
   That out of sorrow might be born the joy,
His fully then, when all those foès are sharing,
   Whose angry enmity he would destroy?

Oh, heart, look up, for, see, aloft is shining
   The great prophetic City of His Love;
Saints with Himself the Saviour is combining,
   That by one work below, one rest above
For people and king may be for ever gained;
   Into its joy each saddened song returns,
Nor friend nor foe need any more be pained,
   When heaven's one fire in every bosom burns.

CHAPTER XIII.

SPIRITUAL HINTS,

A CURTAIN Difficulty is,
Meeting and hindering the gaze ;
Rise, and lift it with your hand,
Then the eye may look beyond ;
What to Thought a veil must prove,
That an action may remove ;
Thus by Doing you shall know
What it is you have to do.

———•———

If thy mind be like a tree, which roots as it grows,
And thy heart be like a river, which widens as it flows,
Then thy will may be a wind, which strengthens as it
blows.

———•———

Every man is his own straight gate.

We are not free, but free to be made free.

The wisest habit is the habit of care in the
formation of habits.

When the ship shakes, do not throw yourself into the sea. When storms of doubt assault spiritual truth, do not abandon yourself to the wild evil of the world that "cannot rest." The ship rolls in the wind, but by the wind advances.

While the heart beats, it will sometimes throb.

———◆———

Unsettled, imperfect opinions may be the flickerings of our expiring lamp of truth; or they may be young callow birds, now unsightly, that will presently become as Sacred Convictions, birds feathered and of song.

———◆———

It was Trinal's custom to take long walks. This chapter, and indeed this book, is partly the result of them. Some of these were by a river, the very name of which we should be ashamed to tell: for some of our readers perhaps have been up the Rhine, or even up the Mississippi. Nevertheless, he loved that river; and maintained, too, that a field of new-blown buttercups was one of the fairest as well as most golden sights that earth can offer. He thought this sight even "glorious." But as almost every thing is called "glorious," from a cranberry-pie up to a tropical sunset, that, perhaps, is not surprising. His note-books bear many evidences of these walks. Whimsical things, sometimes, are entered, when it is evident enough that his general thought had been strenuous, tinged, too, with sadness. Selections from the shorter of these entries might be variously grouped, in Trinal's manner, as "Groves," "Gardens of Herbs," "Flower Gardens," "Spiritual Hints." Some of the spiritual hints are given above. But the rest of the chapter contains a selection, under the generally appropriate title of—

NOTES FOR THE CONSIDERATE.

THE LION IN LOVE.

It is fabled that the lion fell in love, and was sick of love; so he went to the father of the damsel, and demanded his daughter for a wife. But the father said he could not hear of such a thing, unless the lion would consent to have his teeth drawn and his claws broken. To this the lion, being so sick of love that he was foolish, consented. Now, when his teeth were drawn and his claws broken, the man fell upon him with a club and beat out his brains; and thus, his suit prospering, he lost his life. Truth is of lion-like energy, and has lion-like defences. The world has a daughter named Favour, whom Truth loves. " Give me your Favour," says Truth to the World. The World, to entrap the adversary, feigns consent. "Lay aside your sternness and your strength, and my Favour shall be yours." So lion-like Truth, sick of desire for the world's favour, yields up his defences, and then, helpless against his disguised enemy, is despoiled of his life.

WINE AND FUNGUS.

A certain man had in his cellar choice wine. It remained there long, carefully locked up. The wine being needed, they sought it in the cellar, but the door could not be opened. So it was broken through, and the cellar was seen to be filled with tough fungus. The wine was all gone, and this huge growth of fungus was its transmutation. The choice wine is spiritual truth, which we carefully lock up for safety in the cellar called Creed. The wine being wanted to strengthen or comfort us, we find the door of the cellar shut against us, and soon discover to our dismay that the wine has changed into that tough, disgusting fungus called Cant.

THE BOTTLE, OR THE FOUNTAIN?

Is it better for a man to be as a bottle, out of which you may pour the little water that could be poured in ; or as a fountain, which gathers waters from sources far or near, and has always a supply? Shall we reject the waters of the fountain, because they receive from the ground through which they rise a mineral taste? It may not be desirable that all waters should have this taste, but very important that some should, for such waters may be specially salutary in many painful sicknesses.

THE GOOD AND THE BETTER.

The better often springs from the good, as a green shoot from a seed, the covering of which it breaks, and the substance of which it exhausts, that its own growth may have free course and nourishment. The seed perhaps is beautiful, with a shining ornamented surface. Shall we call it spoiling the seed when the fresh shoots break through this surface and then con-

sume the substance ?   Shall we call the better
the foe of the good, because it absorbs it to
live by it ?   Yet some would have us keep the
forms of truth taught us, as seeds in a drawer ;
and if we plant them in our mind, and growth
begins, they are angry because the seed is
spoiled ! So also policies and institutions are
bewailed, and the better ones, which rise from
them and absorb all the good they possessed,
arc considered as destroying them.   There are
those who allow that we should sow, but say
ever, The time is not come.   But when we feel
deeply, it is our spring-tide, and unless we plant
then, the season will pass, and the seed remain
perhaps but to moulder and perish.

THE NAPKIN AND THE SACK.

Dost thou believe this doctrine that I ask
thee of ?   Dost thou hold it firmly ?   Indeed I
do, sir.   I keep it most carefully.   Keep it carefully ! What dost thou mean ?   I have it, sir,
folded away in a napkin.   A napkin ! What is
the name of that napkin ?   It is called Secret
Doubt.   And why dost thou keep the truth in
the napkin of secret doubt ? They tell me that,
if exposed to the air of inquiry, it will disap-

pear ; so when asked for it I shall not have it, and shall perish. Thou art foolish, and they that have told thee this are foolish. Truth is corn, and thou wilt not be asked for the corn first given thee, but for sheaves. Thou art as if keeping thy corn in the sack of unbelief. The corn shall be taken from thee if thou use it not, and thyself put in thy sack of unbelief, and drowned in the deep, as evil-doers were punished in old times.

THE INJURED CHRYSALIS.

A man had for his god a chrysalis. Its life was wonderful to him, but he knew not its powers. Coming one morning to it, he found the chrysalis a broken and empty case, and near it saw a large-winged, bright-eyed creature very beautiful. This, said he, is Satan as an angel of light ; wretch! thou hast devoured my god. Then he struck the creature with his hand and killed it. So the perfect life perished, because it was believed it had destroyed the imperfect life that was so much honoured. Thus it is when truth and goodness present themselves in their highest forms, they are not recognized by those who so much honour the lower

s

forms through which they must pass. They are treated as destroyers of these, and their own destruction is sought.

VENTILATION.

When a man complains of winds of doctrine, who is to blame, he or the winds? Things easily movable may be driven about, not because the winds are so strong, but because themselves are so light. Some men are as spiritual invalids; we must kindly grant them allowance. But their weakness must not limit the useful and necessary exercise of other men's liberty. We may so shrink from wind that we may become afraid of air. And often, by application of rules based on our own natural or imposed necessities, we may afflict the constitution of those under our control with dangerous sickliness, or bring upon them a most insalutary dread of exposure. The mind needs air of thought and wind of inquiry to keep all its chambers pure and sweet, and its powers vigorous.

CASTLES, SWORDS, AND THE PLOUGHSHARE.

Old creeds may be like old castles, venerable

memorials of stirring times that have happily
passed. Strong were the walls now mouldering,
and strong must have been the men that built
and that defended them ; but they speak of
war and troubles. And so, large and decisive
in plan and expression are these old creeds,
and strong spiritual men were they out of whose
hearty thought they grew, and by whose soul
in zeal they were held and defended. But in
their strength there is a grim sternness. And,
as we need not now build castles, neither need
we now frame such creeds as these. It is better
to live a comfortable and neighbourly life in
our separate and various Homes of Opinion,
than to share in common a dangerous life of
battle in the Castles of Creed. Yet without
these castles the quieter life could not have
been secured. And the Church may really be
as proud of its creeds as the nation of its
castles. We may keep spiritual books of a
bygone time on our shelves, as rusty sword-
blades are sometimes kept hanging over the
mantlepieces in our houses. They are heir-
looms, not now for service, yet cherished memorials of services once rendered, and rendered
faithfully. Books have been, have needed to be,
and still need to be often as swords. Yet the

theologic sword must be beaten into the theologic ploughshare. Churches must not flash
their creeds, as carefully tempered steel swords,
in each other's faces, and in the faces of the
people; but, fashioning them into ploughshares,
open up great furrows in the public heart, that
the seeds of good works for personal and social
advantage may be sown plentifully.

SPIRITUAL ASSOCIATION.

Our religious life, as so much separatists,
resembles rather a village life with its envy and
scandal, than a city life with its frank confidence, with its individual liberty, numerous
lesser associations, and grand general combinations for the public good. Yet separatists who
love union are its best friends, though their
labour for it is painful. In setting the house
of the Church in order, they are compelled to
begin with displacings and confusion, and to
endure them and work amidst them long. There
is hope that we are drawing nearer to a life
that may be represented by the city life; when
the Church Catholic will not be the large gar-
nished sepulchre of truth, but the ordered and
populous city of God. Our motto has seemed

this—"No more temples for the world, but every man an oratory in his own garden." Would that all men had an oratory in the garden of their heart! But let every man be rather both a temple and a single stone for that greater temple—the Church. Let his perfecting of himself be, that he may be built up with "saints" upon the foundation of prophets and apostles, Christ being the corner-stone.

SPRINGS AND RAINDROPS.

The individual, in relation to the multitude of human influences that act upon him, is as a spring to many raindrops; but, in relation to another individual mind, as a raindrop to a spring. What an infinite number of the thoughts and acts of other men must there have been, for our life to be, in fulness and quality, what it is; and we ourselves, as members of the great social company, by what we do and think, form part of that great rain of influence by which other springs are flowing, or shall rise. Every man is both a son of the Race and a Father of Posterity. His life is born of the general life of the world, and the good or evil of the world that shall be, must in part take origin from him.

TIMBER AND TREE.

All timber was once Tree.   Before it was
hewn for use it was compacted by life.   The
free-growing, spiritual thought of one generation
or century fashions materials for the usages and
institutions of the next.   The beams of cathe-
drals, the rafters of our houses, planks in the
ship, and posts by the wayside,—who can say in
what wild forests, or what dizzy mountain-sides,
or in what retired valleys the trees were nourished whence all these have been fashioned ?
There are people too, whom wisdom as well as
whim may call—wooden. They are not so much
saplings from old trees, as they are timbers
which owe their solidity to these old trees. They
have strength and worth, but they have little
originative life. So it is, that the descendants of
spiritual persons, the modern representatives of
old spiritual societies, possess what we may call
so much ready-made character.   What there is
now of spiritual life amid their forms and usages,
is rather as air which keeps a log from the dry
rot, than as air which, stirring among the boughs
of a tree, nourishes life.

THE BIBLE AND THE NEWSPAPER.

The newspaper would be but a poor substitute for the Bible; but if we make the newspaper representative of actual human experiences and strivings, and the Bible representative of that spiritual wisdom according to which human life progresses onward towards a certain general end; then we may say, That he reads his Bible with little heart and for little purpose who does not study his newspaper, and that he reads his newspaper for an excitement sure to issue in vanity and disappointment who does not study his Bible. Truth gives to life interpretation and hope; life gives to truth new reality and impressiveness.

MAGNETIC MUD.

It is found in some of the American lakes, that the boats are strangely hindered in their progress. They are drawn downwards, and the use of the oar is difficult, and this is because of the magnetic power of deep mud concealed below the surface of the waters. So is it in the lives of men and the life of the world. Good works are vessels that cannot advance without difficulty over the waves of life ; heavy are their movements, and they seem to be sinking as they move : and this is because of old evil, which, as mud, has slowly gathered.   There must be purgation ; and new proclaimings and enforcings of truth must become as the powerful, cleansing flow of a great stream.

THE WORLD'S TROUBLES.

A new speaker of truth is as an angel sent by God to trouble the waters of thought, and after the troubling there is healing for those who first step in.   For some few years or generations the waters retain their efficacy, but then again need a new troubling by some prophet or wise man. When Christ came, He permanently troubled the waters of the world's life, yet ever and anon there have needed to be minor troublings.

COLUMBUS AND HIS SAILORS.

As the sailors of Columbus were to him in his voyage of discovery, so are our faculties to us in the endeavour of our spirit, and so to the witness for truth are his fellow-men in the work to which he has called them.   The sailors said, " Where is the land?" and again, "Where is the land ?" When the continuing east wind—the trade wind—blew, it seemed to the sailors an omen of fear—" Will it not blow us on and on and on for ever ?" So in the advance of the mind in the search of spiritual or political truth and good, or even in the pursuit of sciences. The impulse of a great directive thought, though it is as a wind from God—His trade wind, which will conduct us to, and then facilitate our inter-course with some new and now to be discovered land—produces, as we are advanced onward, distrust and fear. Though our faculties heartily were with us at the first, and though our fellow-men entered the ship of endeavour with pride and hope, yet now is there anger. The captain is called fool. It is asked, " Where is the land ? This sea is endless, and the wind will blow us on over it for ever and for ever."

SPECIAL KNOWLEDGE AND GENERAL IMPRESSION.

Two sorts of persons are to be alike avoided—those who offer you explanation of every thing, and those who care not for full explanation of any thing. They are alike mischievous. The uninquiring, if they profess regard for truth, hold it in ignorance; its virtues are as those of a valued, but unexamined, charm. They are dead in habits and prejudices, and so in trespasses and sins. They who would explain all, and make so-called explanation of truth equivalent to its possession as a power of life, are noisy, vain, and unserviceable. They reverence not the Holy. They know not that the Divine love dwells in the cloudy tabernacle of the Divine wisdom; that light may yet be light inaccessible. He to whom much is clear and much dark, is as one who sees that the water of a well is pure and transparent, though the bottom is hidden from him. He can see into that which he cannot see through. It is not the darkness, but the muchness of the water, that hinders the eye from penetrating. Truths, presenting themselves as flourishing but tangled growths in country places, may do the heart good by their beauty, before they have been recognized in their distinctness and traced to their origin. Yet we should seek to distinguish the several sorts of leaf and blossom, and acquaint ourselves with the properties of these, and of their roots. Till we look we do but imperfectly see; but, as we imperfectly see, we may so feel as to induce careful looking; and when we have looked, we shall both know and feel freshly how admirable the growths are in their differences and their blending.

THE EMOTIONAL IN MAN.

The swell and influence of different emotional states, that are not in any just correspondence with truths known or labours to be done, yet indicate the greatness of man. Excessive joy, sorrow, or fear, rather represent the boundless capacities there are in man for loving, grieving, and fearing, than assure us that there is some present experience to which they are but adequately proportioned. Fanaticisms are the sudden blazings up of loose-textured minds. Like loose, dry bushes, these are on fire in an instant, burn rapidly, expire, then smoke awhile. Strong minds are like firm-grained wood, which kindles slowly, but burns long. Yet these fanaticisms show us how the human emotion enlarges itself as to infiniteness. They are hyperboles of the feelings—very dangerous from their vague vastness; yet to the wise they are discoveries of what is in man, that contain prophecy of what shall be in the world. They are unreasonal sweepings of great waves of the soul, upheaved from its rest, as by earthquake beneath; they show the mightiness of the sea, but it is a might that desolates. Enthusiasms, which represent the infinitude of truth, and the greatness of man, feeling the truth and impelled by it, are rather like the irrepressible risings of great tidal waves, resistless, but measured and slow.

THE CLEVER AND THE WISE.

Cleverness is as dexterity of the fingers—only of worth when under the control of kindness and wisdom. Talent may weave snares, or it may frame apparel; and skill is, so to speak, a satisfaction to the fingers, whether its devices be evil or good. Talent may occupy itself in unravelling difficulties that vex and ensnare, or in forming intricate knots to puzzle. There is a temper of mind inventive of doubts, and the cleverness in which it orginates is as dexterity of finger without wisdom of heart. But doubt that arises necessarily in a life of right endeavour and desire is one of the best moral indications, though to pass through it be one of the most painful moral processes. If doubt show an awakened mind, unsatisfied with assent of the lip and notional furnishing of the head—an earnest hungering for truth, that life may be ordered honestly and confidingly by its rule, then is it a token for

good. Wise observance of the time may show
us whether there are circumstances likely to produce a large class of doubters whose moral state
is good; but to determine of individuals whether
they belong to this class, we must carefully "try
their spirits"—note which way the current of their
affection and endeavour is setting. For if "wise
in heart" they will "receive commandments."

DISCIPLESHIP.

"Articles of Faith" should be as "Articles
of Apprenticeship " — Apprenticeship to the
Truth.

If we know that we have as yet but imperfectly
learned the things that we believe, and desire
that their character and faculty may be more
fully unfolded for us; then they are as a chosen
company of affectionate disciples, of distinct
characters and fit for distinct offices, agreeing to
learn together of one master, the Truth, and
sitting at his feet in reverent trust and dependence. But if we be loud, vain, and stubborn,
then the things we believe are a rabble of Asser-
tions, that come forth with the dark-lantern of
Prejudice and the club of Bigotry, to seize and
bind the Truth, betrayed thus to bondage and

death, so far as we have power of death, by the Judas of our Worldly Policy.

LATITUDINARIANISM.

There is a wise and an unwise latitudinarianism. The one results from shallowness of heart and superficiality of knowledge; the other from deepness of heart and profundity and variety of investigations. The one tolerates any thing, because all things seem much alike; the other recognizes the true every where, because all things have dependency on deep, inward, controlling causes. The wise latitudinarian is also an altitudinarian: his thought spreads broadly, but it is also high-rising, and strikes deep.

AN ERA.

Thoroughly to settle a thought, so that it may have practical efficacy in our life, requires long time usually. But if there be a time when we specially receive and affirm to ourselves some great truth, having clear vision of its royalty, and earnestly purposing allegiance, such a time constitutes an era in our history. Well is it when we know that we are called to warfare, and resolve to serve; know also that our chief victory must be over ourself, and that this conquest will not be achieved by one pitched battle, but by a war of slow subjugation—a campaign comprising many battles.

SPARKS AND FIRE.

We may set our foot on a spark, but we cannot trample out a conflagration : so by the energy of our will we may repress first risings of evil ; but we cannot overcome evil dispositions. The wisest decision of our will is to seek alliance with the Supreme Will. He who is the Supreme Will is the Supreme Goodness. He works not alone for us, but with us—supplying us with energy of holy life, with His own good Spirit. By the "Spirit of God" may we quench the "spirit of the world"—the fire that ravages ; and then by the "word of truth" rebuild what has been thus made waste and desolate. As partakers of the holy life, we have strengthening dispositions by which we work, according to directive thoughts ; and, becoming heedful, we hinder many sparks from breaking out into fires. Evil gradually we thus overcome by good.

THE CANDLE AND THE LAMP.

If you carry a candle with you in the open air,

you have to cover the flame with your hand, and to keep your eye upon it ; any wind may blow it out. But a lamp is safe from the wind ; and, if you carry it, your eye is left free. Truth that you only acknowledge, and have not secured by the habit of your life, is like the flame of the candle. You wish the aid of its light to guide you when out in dark places of the world ; but, in order to shield it, you have so to look to it that you cannot see by it. Any wind of opposing influence may extinguish it. Put your thought into a habit, and instead of a flaring candle you will have a steady lamp.

WILFULNESS AND KNOWLEDGE.

Wilfulness fails often, as the struggles of a man do who strives to open a door with a wrong key. He is strong, but he is wrong. A right thought is as a true key. But though it is the true key, he who has it may need all his strength ; for the door may be a heavy one, and the lock rusted. It is often alike vain to be wilful without being wise ; and to have knowledge, without having also patience and resolute will.

THE ABUNDANCE OF THE HEART.

Out of the abundance of the heart the mouth speaketh ; and our best abundance of the heart must be slowly and in quietness prepared. The cattle when they rest are yet working to prepare from the grass that sweetest and most wholesome of beverages—milk. So must we prepare the abundance of the heart. If the milk of our word is to flow from us nourishingly, we must turn the common things of daily life—the grass— by slow and quiet processes, into sweet wisdom. In retired, meditative hours, the digesting and secreting powers of the spirit act ; and thus ourselves are nourished, and we store nourishment for others.

SELF-REVISION.

Housekeepers, by frequent inspections and attention, preserve the brightness of their furniture and utensils. Because of this daily carefulness, the house does not need often to be "turned out of windows." So must we keep our habits and principles bright and serviceable, if the house of our spirit is to be a comfortable home, and its furnishings beautiful and dear to us. We shall not need great and frequent disturbance of

T

our inward life, if we practise daily order and self-revision.

DISCONTENT.

There is a discontent which is the child of pride and idleness. It seeks for its comfort the bed of the sluggard, and lies there till its whole skin is chafed, and its every bone sore ; and envy is its communing with its own heart upon its bed. But sometimes the discontent of a man is as the choking gas which rises from the snuff of a common candle. It indicates that the powers of his nature, which would feed light, are being wasted. Some wild wind of misfortune, perhaps, has extinguished the flame of his free-burning spirit. A well-directed breath, or the touch of a taper— a word of encouragement, or a connexion with one who is giving forth calmly the light of his work or thought—may rekindle this man's light. Thus, discontent may indicate both what a man has suffered and what he can do. And if we can remove it, we both benefit him and increase the sum of good influences. For he who burns, shines; and by his shining, general light is increased.

FAULT AND DISEASE.

There is seldom diseasedness of character in

which there is not something of fault; and seldom
fault in which there is not something of disease.
Infirmity is as the soil on which sin grows ; and
when the evil plant is plucked up, there remains
a quality in the soil which weakens good ones,
lessening their beauty, fragrance, and fruitfulness.
Besides, sins are many-seeded, and it is with
them as with various common weeds; whilst at
the top of any one stem there are flowers not yet
opened, beneath are others in their full bloom, and
at the bottom are ripe seeds.   It is difficult then
to extirpate sin from a congenial soil.   So is
infirmity related to sin, that often our great fear
is, lest infirmities should pass into sins; and often
the only hope we dare entertain is, that where
sin was, infirmity alone may show itself.

THE DIVINE SPIKENARD.

The breaking of the body of Christ, His death,
was as the breaking of the alabaster box of very
precious ointment—not a waste lavishing, but a
free giving of a most costly gift.   The odour of
sacrificing love has for our health and exhilaration, diffused itself through the air of all lands.
Wherever the word of the Gospel comes, this
enlivening and restoring fragrance " bewrayeth

itself." Sense of good, in sorrows endured in love, for the truth and according to the will of God, is like sweet spicy air wafted to us from lands yet afar off, whilst we are tossing our way towards them over the deep. Such fragrant wind of life is "the word of the truth of the Gospel."

WORKING THE PUMPS.

When the vessel has sprung a leak, and the sailors are engaged in working the pumps, the ship cannot make much way over the waters. To keep afloat is the great thing. If the haven shall be at last reached, yet the advance of the voyage must be retarded. Often when we are expecting activity from an individual, such as would be like the happy progress of a voyaging ship, we find, on inquiry, that he is working the pumps. The tempest has been upon him, and the waters have broken in through leaks of Disappointment, Sickness, and Bereavement. It is much if he can but keep afloat ; and if he can advance some little, that is his utmost. The time is one of anxiety, but of labour, strenuous labour, too.

HOW TO BUILD AN ARK.

He that would build an ark of safety to bear

him up over the boisterous waters of Transiency, must fashion it of great beams of Necessity: that necessity which is Eternal Wisdom's purpose.

PLEASURE AND THANKS.

The vine of pleasure does not yield clusters of the finest, richest sort, unless it grows in an atmosphere often moistened by the rains of sorrow. But the rains must not be perpetual. And pleasures that we have through pain will give fresh sweetness to pleasures without pain; but we must have these too. The relish of the cup is not alone in the wine, but in the drinker, and he has it from a thirsty and a thankful heart. Yet there must be the wine, though thirst and thankfulness give the relish. God withholds the cup sometimes that it may be the sweeter. But when we drink and are glad, our merry heart is not our sin but our sacrifice—the sacrifice of our gratitude. Have we a pleasure? Have we built a nest? Is health firm, are friends kind, and earthly comforts like silver in Solomon's days for plenty? Then let us eat and drink heartily, for it is God who has made the food of the body, the eye, the ear, and the heart pleasant. But let us eat and drink temperately, for if to-day we live on earth, to-morrow we may live in heaven.

If earthly comforts be as silver in Solomon's days for plenty, let them also, like silver in his days, be nothing accounted of by reason of the gold. If, sometimes, all that is within us, all the company of our affections, makes merry as with many instruments of music, let our song of Love and Faith towards God, like the voice of a great singer towering above all the band and the chorus, sound forth and be heard as sweeter and stronger than all the melody of our earthly joy, in full unison with it, yet with supremacy over it, giving to it nobleness and a crown.

CHAPTER XIV.

OUR last was a prose chapter, this will be a verse one. Some sedate pieces introduce others slighter and almost sportive. But Theophilus says, "Why should not solemnity be wanting, when it is not wanted?" The chapter ends, however, with a piece duly grave and moral on that Procrastination which is "the thief of time"— a thief often condemned, but always out in the world on "ticket-of-leave," and continually doing again to-day as he did yesterday, that is to say, doing nothing—except mischief. The magnificence, wisdom, and invincibleness of King Cras, and the flourishing state of his dominions are in this poem set forth.

THE WIFE'S BIRTHDAY.

Heart! have you any thing of verse
　　To greet the birthday of a wife?
Tender the words must be, but terse,
　　Suiting the common sense of life;
Rank'd in an honest, steady line,
With nothing false and nothing fine:

But plain and sweet, to please a soul
   Of true love's own simplicity;
The parts consistent with the whole,
   The whole such as may company
Or with a prayer, or a kiss—
Heart! can you give me verse like this?

Affection's strength you need not prove—
   An overproof suggests pretence—
By warm elaborate words of love,
   But with a modest confidence,
Enough, if you will for me say,
" We are more wedded every day."

Count the full years we've been together,
   And lest she cry, " Ah, full of care!"
Tell her that soon the winter weather
   Will soften now, and spring's repair
Bring back to cheer the wayside places
Primroses with their golden faces.

Speak of the sure immortal light,
   And say the mortal heart resembles
Unsteady water, which, though bright,
   Is bright but with a beam that trembles
That faith must tremulously shine,
And yet it is a light divine.

Hint piously that souls akin
   Shall some day one another meet,
And that an early-parted twin
   More blest may be, in heaven sweet,
For gentle, secret service kind,
Done to the brother left behind.

Say, too, that though Time drives the years,
　God rules the paces and the path,
Oft checks the course for human fears,
　And garments warm provided hath:
And as we through the stages come,
We near the gate of distant home.

O Heart! can you provide me verse
　To say this, and the day to bless?
And better health, a fuller purse,
　Some unexpected happiness,
These wish, too, for the day's return—
Then, Heart, my gratitude you earn.

" These very words of your request,"
　My heart replied, " these offer her;
To verse the choicest and the best
　Such words of love she will prefer ;
In husband's talk unto his heart
The true wife ever would have part."

THE SINGER.

"Sing praises unto God, sing praises."

I heard the winter weep and sob
　Through hours of a moonless night,
When the blank fields and naked trees
　Were suffering the wind's despite :
And yet, as on my bed I lay,
　My heart, she sang in her delight.

With change of weeks now shone the moon,
  Her beam of double pureness bright
Shining on self-illumined snows
  That help'd her beautify the night:
And still, as on my bed I lay,
  My heart, she sang in her delight.

So sings she on calm summer days,
  When even the very grass is still;
And when the winds that herald showers
  Sound from the woods, she singeth still.
All times, she saith, their music have;
  And sing she must, and sing she will!

She finds a glory in the dark,
  Another glory in the sun;
A glory in the ending year,
  A glory in the spring begun;
And thus her changeful, steady song
  She sings, as round the seasons run.

JANUARY VERSES.

The rough, dark-visaged winter,
  Lord of each icy wind,
Is a lover of the beautiful,
  And has a warm heart kind.

He fashions snow-flakes delicate,
  He gives the drift its curl;
He breathes a charm, and magic winds
  Make the black trees bright with pearl.

His icy-finger'd frost-power—
    Gentle as it is strong—
Fetters the river flow, and weaves
    Ice-lace the sides along.

In a solemn muse he paces
    The silence-haunted pole,
And thoughts of wonder and pity and love
    Make music in his soul.

Then he besweeps the world with wind
    Of soft and sorrowful tone,
That the listening heart of man may hear
    A music like his own.

And oft he comes where families
    In the fire-shine circle round,
Telling the tale of wonder and hope,
    And love that sought and found.

And frost-forms on his fancy crowd
    Even as he stops to listen ;
Then of story-breath he weaves the flowers
    That on the windows glisten.

He stands with the lonely student,
    Up-gazing through the air,
At solemn heaven circling slow
    Round the ever fixèd star.

The north sky he makes merry bright,
    Light upon light advances
To change and vanish, as in a heart,
    Bright bewildering fancies.

With cold snow the world he whitens,
  Spreads clearest blue above,
Earth and the heaven agreeing fair,
  Like purity and love.

And winter looks for coming spring,
  As age for a daughter mild;
And hopes to die with his old white head
  Reposed upon his child.

THE PRAISE OF NOVEMBER,

November, honour'd by the few,
  Though hated by the unthinking many,
'Tis hard that all the months but you
  Should have their praise, and you not any!

Fine things they say of April showers,
  April, who hailstones at us throws;
Her blue skies and her blue-bell flowers;
  Pshaw!—nothing's blue except one's nose

There's March will only snarl and fret;
  Instead of rushing like a warrior
To drive off February's wet,
  He cheats our hopes and leaves us sorrier.

The blooming May is sleety too,
  And June as cold as any beauty;
Indeed, there's scarce a month but you
  That can be found to do its duty.

Thus if we want a Christmas snow,
  In vain we trust to old December;
'Tis seen in picture books, I know—
  Who can a *real* white day remember?

January's frosts are all pretences,
  Two days or three, and then a thaw;
You lose your temper and your senses
  At such a fickle month and raw.

Poor February gets much abuse,
  Yet is of early months the best;
Does dirty work that's full of use,
  And finishes before the rest.

July? Oh! yes, July is bright—
  A passionate and selfish lover,
Who, kind for days of brief delight,
  Can frown and thunder when they're over.

August is good, but rather dull,
  Brings sometimes weeks of mopy weather:
September's harvest 's seldom full,
  But fails in part, or altogether,

October is serene and fair,
  But being fair, deceit attends her;
She's fine awhile, then soon the air
  Grows damp, and brings the influenza.

Let other months then—praised enough!
  Own tardy justice to their brother;
And blamed for once, accept reproof,
  And mend and comfort one another.

His wind, perhaps, is sometimes rough,
　　For that a coat will make provision;
His fog is wholesome kind of stuff,
　　And suits an English disposition.

In balminess, his finer days
　　Exceed the finest days of June;
Lights softer than the summer's blaze,
　　Sounds quieter than autumn's tune

Has he; and skies so pale, so tender,—
　　Like violets which in lonely places
Appealingly their beauty render,
　　And bring our love into our faces.

A pathos is there in November;
　　With many an hour hush'd and clear
He heals the wounds we long remember,
　　And mourns the battle of the year.

Healing he speaks of conflict yet,
　　And mourns, but whispering still of peace,
Hope sympathises with regret,
　　Life sacredly defies decease.

WORDS.

Oh! sweet, sweet words, that tenderly besprinkle
　　Our best affections with a sunny rain,
Gentle as winds that scarce the waters wrinkle,
　　Or bend the grasses on the meadowy plain.

Wise is the lady that can add your sweetness
  To the pure quiet of her smiling eyes,
And all the household forms of graceful neatness
  That her ingenious busy hand supplies :
Still from her heart, the flower, her voice, the bee
  Brings honey forth, and murmurs pleasantly.

HEAR THE WEATHERCOCK!

A weathercock perch'd up on high,
While turning in the gusty sky,
Spake thus, in loud soliloquy,
Fickle is all the world but I :

"Even the very clock below
Is sometimes fast and sometimes slow ;
But look at me and you will know
Exactly how the wind may blow.

"Why, all the stars begin to fly
When little fleecy clouds run by ;
But steadfast through the night am I.
And serve my master faithfully.

"Obedient, I turn any way,
At any hour of night or day,
And never mind what people say
Who wish the wind to go or stay ;

"No, not the girls so nicely drest,
Nor farmers, for the crops distrest,
Who always fancy *they* know best,
And *will* look north, though I look west.

"Old Hodge, that hobbles on his stick,
Old Susan, of the ague sick,
Old Lady Grumbles, with the tick,
Would like the warmest winds to pick;

" But storms I neither seek nor shun,
I glisten in the evening sun,
Or darken ere the day is done—
And down by me the lightnings run.

" I'm wet with rain or white with snow,
Or ruddy with the morning glow;
I love the gales that noisiest grow,
And clouds that darkest shadows throw.

" The sun his brightest smiles may try—
I shall not turn for him, not I !
The Wind's my Master, and that's why
I wait upon his lightest sigh:

" And let him bluster from the sea,
Or whisper from the grassy lea—
Come as he will he pleases me,
I am the pink of constancy ! "

PROVIDENCE.

The very hairs upon our head are number'd,
    And noticed in the change from bright to gray;
For God with multitude is not encumber'd,
    Well knows each atom what his voice doth say;
Why then so fearful are we, ever counting
    Our cares, our enemies, our troubles over;
Perplexing silly self with sums amounting
    Unto a total only God can cover ?

Who from the dusty road would miss a sparrow,
 Or in a garden hear one chirp the less ?
Kind as our hearts may be our views are narrow,
 But God each thing can notice and can bless:
With careful love He gives the humblest creatures
 Their tiny cups of brimful happiness,
And makes them in their turns impressive preachers
 Of faith, hope, charity, and good success.

He clothes the rugged rocks with tender mosses,
 He floats the lilies on the water's brim ;
He is chief Shepherd, and each lamb that crosses
 The mountain steep is led and fed by Him ;
He gives the butterfly and flower their beauty—
 His promise in a parable they speak
To all who will fulfil the simple duty
 Of trusting Him, and heavenly glory seek.

There is no searching of His understanding,
 From stars to grasses He extends His care ;
And weary spirits on the bright shore landing,
 Find all they want is known and ready there:
We live for heaven, but earth, too, has its blessing ;
 If more in worth the jewel than the casket,
Yet God keeps both : our soul His grace possessing.
 Corn for the body will not fail our basket.

PROOFS.

The man that can and will
 In the rough waters swim,
And calmly keep his courage still—
 We know the proof of him.

U

The man by praise unbought,
And free from haste and whim,
Who speaks aloud his inward thought—
We know the proof of him.

The man who hails the morn,
While yet with dazzling rim
The day's new monarch is unborn—
We know the proof of him.

The man who not for gold
His way will wind and trim,
But rich or poor is just and bold—
We know the proof of him.

The man who will not plead
His weary head and limb,
When love is at its sorest need—
We know the proof of him.

The man who hates excess,
Yet fills up to the brim
His every cup of kindliness—
We know the proof of him.

The man who fears no cry
Of party-bigot grim,
But meekly stands, and sturdily—
We know the proof of him.

The man whose laughter rings
A puzzle to the prim :
Yet who no witty poison flings—
We know the proof of him,

The man who plunging dives
Where others only skim,
And so at real truth arrives—
We know the proof of him.

The man who brightly shines,
Not flickering and dim,
But steady as the heavenly signs—
We know the proof of him.

This man for our behoof,
In body stout or slim,
Hath manfully wrought out the proof—
That God hath wrought in him.

KING CRAS.

King Cras on his deceitful throne
    Sits gravely hearing cases;
But judgment he will still postpone
    Amid the moral faces
Of courtiers, who every one
    Can logically say,
Why what is pleading to be done
    Should not be done to-day.

King Cras, though he is threaten'd oft
    With certain deposition,
By always speaking people soft
    Can change their disposition:
He promises them much and well,
    Proposes novel schemes;
If they begin their woes to tell,
    King Cras, he tells his dreams.

King Cras, he likes to hear the cries,
   Of any one aspirant,
" Rebellion let us organize,
   Our king, he is a tyrant ! "
Full well he knows he is exempt
   From cause of fear and sorrow,
When told the rebels their attempt
   Have put off till to-morrow.

King Cras has his peculiar way
   Of valuing time present ;
He eats and drinks and laughs to-day,
   Does all that he finds pleasant :
He has besides his daily work ;
   This work, it is—to borrow ;
But other business he will shirk—
   He leaves it till to-morrow.

King Cras, he has a palace vast,
   So rapid was the building,
That from the rougher work they pass'd
   At once unto the gilding.
To-day must every nerve be strain'd
   To make the gilding grand :
To-morrow might be ascertain'd
   Whether the walls would stand.

King Cras is so magnificent,
   Expensive is his budget ;
But when he meets his Parliament
   They're never found to grudge it :

His *dearest* project is their pet,
  They feel no hesitation,
Pleased to increase the public debt—
  The sole wealth of the nation.

Approach the city of King Cras,
  And strange is the illusion,
All fair and stately seems, whereas
  All's ruin and confusion;
Mansions have but a gate and tower
  A church is but a steeple ;
And roofless houses every hour
  Come tumbling on the people.

King Cras has many travellers
  To visit his dominions,
With whom he readily confers,
  And gives them his opinions;
Their interests, he'll make his own,
  He says, and they believe him,
And very few of them are known
  Who ever after leave him.

King Cras, he swaggers and cajoles,
  But, it must be confest
Rules over miserable souls,
  Tormented with unrest ;
Some with a cureless palsy sigh,
  Some of despair are dying ;
The bitterer the wish to fly
  The less the power of flying.

No land there is, nor any seven—
   Oh, terrible to tell !—
Where people talk so much of heaven
   And feel so much of hell;
No land like Crasland in the earth,
   Where ruinously scatter'd,
Lie minds and hearts of choicest worth
   All broken and bespatter'd.

Crasland, the land of wealth and waste,
   Of laziness and action,
Of mad delay, and madder haste,
   Of boast and of distraction :
Where schemes of plenty and of peace
   In war and famine finish;
And as the nation's hopes increase,
   The grounds of them diminish.

Though all is finery atop,
   All's wretchedness beneath;
Of pleasure there is not a drop
   But is a drop of death :
Each hour as it dribbles past
   A darker sadness tinges;
And there are cruel pangs at last,
   Where first where only twinges.

King Cras, he boldly perseveres
   In promising and sinning;
His remedy for tears and fears
   Is—something new beginning.

All things," he says, with royal smile,
    "To-morrow will be better."
The more with hope he can beguile,
    The heavier will he fetter.

King Cras, he has been oft assail'd
    With Resolutions banded ;
But over millions has prevail'd
    Most doughtily commanded :
His flag of truce possesses charms
    To foil the bold endeavour ;
Captains and men throw down their arms,
    And cry, " King Cras for ever ! "

King Cras was crown'd in ancient days,
    And it is doubtful whether
Until the last consuming blaze,
    He'll vanish altogether :
The sanguine say, " He's ruled so long
    That realm of wreck and sorrow,
His health must now be far from strong,
    Perhaps he'll die—to-morrow ! "

CHAPTER XV.

A RETURN FROM MUSIC.

How dreamily we walk, at night,
  Home from a music sweet!
A ghostly sound the foot arouses,
As you pass the shadowy houses—
  There's no one in the street;
But, perhaps, a woman all alone,
The music of whose life is done.

From some window shines a light;
  Is there one who sleeps,
While a sister or a mother,
Or a father or a brother,
  Tender watching keeps;
And sweet hope, as the hours pass by,
Makes low and distant melody?

In that room where shadows move,
  A mother new may be;
While he who is a father made,
With feeling very strange and glad,
  His little one may see:
And now are baby, man, and wife,
The three-part harmony of life.

Farther on, from high above,
　A student's lamp will beam;
Night-silence is, as if a wind,
Filling the organ of his mind;
　And, like music in a dream,
With many a change of stop and key,
Thought advances wanderingly.

Wakeful, within their silent rooms,
　Some still may musing lie;
And in this middle hush of night,
Perhaps a thought of old delight
　Jars the harp of memory;
And startles every slumbering string,
Sad sounds confused awakening.

But round you, in the darken'd rooms,
　Are families at rest;
Gradual and gentle came repose,
Silently deepening, like the snows;
　Aud now in many a breast
Rules dream-power, with musician's skill,
Guiding the spirit as he will.

The young man of the maiden dreams,
　The maiden dreams of man;
Her treble airiness and grace,
His powerful supporting bass,
　Complete each other can:
Each heart has its peculiar tone,
But none were meant to sound alone.

Your house now in the lamp-shine gleams,
   And, entering, you soon
With head upon your pillow are,
Where, scarcely listening, you hear
   Thought faintly hum its tune;
Like mother who sings child asleep,
Singing on to make the slumber deep.

————•————

In a still chamber at night, when sleepless and in pain, the dim flame of a taper, not one farthing worth, may be as a consoling presence. This "light in a dark place" we give heed to till the day dawns. All comfortable lights are kinsmen of the sun, and the sun is too noble to despise his poor relations. A dim Christian thought may be to us the taper which comforts us whilst we are waiting for the appearance of the day-star —the rising of the Sun of Righteousness. There is a sense in which the fullest answer we can get in this world to questions concerning the way of God, is but as a dawn; and so our faith is a trustful waiting for sunrise. Light is sown for the upright, and in due time they will reap it, if they faint not. But we have not alone to wait patiently for our full sheaves of bright light at the general harvest of lights; we receive many gifts of light now. In God is no darkness at all, and around us are things of His in which is no darkness at all, which walk in brightness, and bear witness that He is light. Such are flowers, beautiful things in their many kinds, music, and the heart's home joys. The beauty of the world and the excellency of God's goodly creatures are to us, when our heart has become an obedient longing heart, as a bright lighthouse on the shore of the eternal, a star of hope and guidance when the sea of life strives. We must not let the roaring of the waves which assaults our ear draw and fix our eye, that we cannot look towards, nay, even fail to see, the lighthouse. The beautiful is both very near us and very far from us. It is near us as the lips of love which we may kiss, and far from us as the solemn but friendly stars. Beauty is as a face, in whose composed benignity you may discern a deep and royal soul, and in whose passing smiles you may read a present and brotherly kindness. We may wonder at the gracious looks of this beauty of the heavens and earth, as men wondered at the gracious words that proceeded from our Saviour's mouth. It is by presence of one Holy Spirit that the heaven graciously gazes, and that Christ graciously spoke and worked.

THE HEAVEN.

Call not the heaven Vacancy—
   Whose colour, soft and deep,
Compels a tear to every eye
   That gazing long will keep;
Whose beauty rests so silently,
   Like a maiden's in a sleep.

O Father great! this heaven high
   Is of Thy love the token;
As sweet and deep as anciently,
   Of stillness yet unbroken;
A love is imaged in the sky,
   Too great to be outspoken.

Our earth, the featured Definite,
   Has meanings all Divine:
But oneness of the Infinite
   Doth in the azure shine;
We seem to see Thee in the height,
   Around we look on Thine.

By works for uses and delight
   We learn Thee part by part;
Thy world reveals to gradual sight
   How manifold Thou art;
But read at once in heaven bright
   Is the fulness of Thy heart.

When gazing on the open blue,
   Our heart and Thine seem near;

Thy love in ours is imaged true,
  As skies in water clear;
Clouds come and pass, but still in view
  The depths of heart appear.

We feel—and all our spirit through,
  As through the air a bell,
Or odour of a blossom new
  Through all a hidden dell,
Spreads joy as deep as heaven's hue,
  Which utterance cannot tell.

TRUTH AND GOOD IN THEIR RELATION.

Sweet is it, from disquieting business, to go forth into the quieting moonlight,—from what seems the heated and narrow prison of our own minds, into the breadth, and coolness, and freshness of the world and the air. Then looking up, we say, " How amiable is this Thy tabernacle, O Lord ! how goodly the tent spread out for the races of mankind to dwell in !" At such a time to ask troubledly the question, What is truth ? seems impossible ; for we are with the truth, and the truth is within us. Yet such times, and all times when deep peace and love and hope are with and within us, are for revelation of truth to us. Truth then says to us, Behold me, possess me. But have we not rather Good at

these times with us? We have good with us,
but good with us is truth with us. Consider
good as that which abides, and on which you
may rely, and it is truth; consider truth as that
which inspires and blesses, and it is good. So
far as we have attained truth, we know Being—
now, Being is ever working—so we know in
Truth, not alone forms of things as parts of the
great form of Being, but the law of their activity,
which is ever producing changes. To know Being
the order of its working, and the purpose of its
working, is to know Truth. Ourselves to be
and to work according to the Divine order and
purpose, is to have the truth in us. Truth is the
light that God hath in Himself—the eternal day-
spring of the Highest One. But with His Light
His Love dwells, and in it His Will acts. The
"entrance of His word" into our hearts, is the
unchangeable light of the unchangeable God
shining into us. Unchangeableness of Love and
Power according to an unchangeable Light—
such is our full apprehension of the Truth of
God. Truth, then, is so dear and venerable a
word to us, because truths are Divine powers for
the good of life—for God acts according to His
thoughts, and His thoughts towards us are for
good and not for evil: we then, knowing a truth,

work by it for ends He approves ; and rejoice in it, for His power is with it.

Whatever affirmations may be made concerning good and the seeking it—these are truths ; the sum of them is our Truth. We cannot know of the world without the senses, nor of Divine good without inward experiences. We must be partakers of the Divine nature in order to know God, as we must have wept, and laughed, and sported, to know the feelings and actions to which these words relate. The love of knowing, and of the knowing endeavour, are to be distinguished from the love of truth—the love of knowing is a good love, but the love of truth is a higher one, including it and limiting it. Truth is the form and the law of good ; and he who loves truth, loves good. And as good is that life of love which is in the whole and for the whole, he who loves truth has no private ends contradictive of general ends.

TRUTH'S COMING AND TRUTH'S RECEPTION.

Truths are sure and unchanging, they are controlling and invincible, they are agreeing and undisturbed. But human affairs, how conflicting they are ! and men, how selfish and how ignorant !

Now, Truth answers for us these questions, What should be done? What may be hoped? And so, because of the state of the world, the holding of truth has often been as the clutch of a spar by a drowning man, or the grasping of a standard in the heat of war. Truths are principal affirmations concerning what is felt and what may be felt, as well as concerning what should be done and may be hoped. To obtain assurance of them, and then to get men to believe them, and work by them, and trust them, is very hard. Great disputes and contradictions, and sorrowful, wondering doubts about truth, will always accompany endeavour for good. All the weakness, the wickedness, and imperfections of men oppose themselves when Truth cries, "I am come a light into the world; he that believeth in me shall not walk in darkness, but shall have the light of life." Always the "form of sound words," Truth, must have in it the spirit of sound life, Good, if it is to be for the world a light of life. When such living words utter themselves, and the spirit that is in them works, among the religious will often be found their great deniers and adversaries. Among the religious will be found the debased fearful, and the bigot and false. Such will become coward haters or envious hinderers of

advancing good. The religious are not necessarily the good, though the fully good are
necessarily religious. None can be fully good
who are not conscious partakers of the Divine
nature; bound, assured, and inspired through
their relation to God. And such are in the
highest sense religious. But all who in word
and habit of life profess themselves God's,
whether it be in selfishness and hypocrisy, or in
love and sincerity, are, though so " mingled "
a people, named—the religious. And among
these bright-faced Truth, standing forth to testify,
will excite in some —hatred, wrath, and jealousy,
seeming to them a reproachful disturber and
destroyer; while by others received with most
affectionate and thankful welcome, as plainly full
of great and heavenly intentions, with words of
promise and of power for the discouraged and the
sorrowful. There is no welcome and communion
like that of the " saints." No odium and wrath,
deadly as those of the men who among the
religious are "showing themselves to be " *the*
religious.

CREED AND CREEDS.

" Word," in the higher sense, is greater than
speech. It needs speech, but must make the

x

speech it needs. The most sacred words, that
is, terms and phrases, which Word once
fashioned and used, may become "offences."
One great reason why change of speech in
regard to "Word," the word of spiritual truth, is
so important, is, because the evil tempers, the
prejudices, and the folly of the speech-users
come to infect their words ; and these vestures of
expressions may no more be safely used than
the garments of the plague-stricken may be
worn. The phraseology has in it the power
of unhealthy states of life, and so not alone is
unserviceable, but noxious. But if we once
apprehend the idea of the word Creed, we
may earnestly affirm Creed to be valuable, nay,
most necessary, when yet particular creeds may
be worthless or mischievous. What then is
Creed ? Creed is the affirmation of spiritual
certainties : *creeds* are sciential expositions of the
relation of these certainties. The Creed that
comprises the most main true affirmations is the
fullest. These affirmations are truths; as truths,
they are powers. A creed may wrongly express
the mutual relations of furtherance and limiting,
that the truth-powers, of which it comprises affirmations, bear to one another. The sciential
exposition—which must be more or less incom-

plete—is made the affirmed certainty; the sum of
affirmed certainties, and of sciential expositions,
is treated as perfect expression of the totality of
certainties and their relations; that is—particular
creeds are made Creed. Then, again : creeds as
expression, being the result of life and of thought
exercised on life, when considered correct and
final, are made rule for the trial and condem-
nation of inquirers who have not yet arrived at
these same results, but who have expressed and
who work by the results at which they have
arrived; or who have arrived at results *inclusive*
of the results expressed in the creed, emendatory
of them, and comprising new affirmations. Truth
is eternal—all the truth-powers that have been,
are now; they may merge for us into higher
truth-powers, and work with one another in
changed ways ; but they cannot die. Therefore,
a portion of each age's results of thought must
remain for after ages. But each age must feel
and think for itself: and therefore, though
absolute Creed is eternal, creeds must be generation after generation new-born. Truth dieth
not, but conviction is in "deaths oft;" and so
Creed has, because of the succession of generations and the fluctuating strife of good and
evil, both new births and resurrections many.

A man may accept phrases and think he is accepting truths; and he may reject truths and think he is rejecting phrases. When phrase is about us infecting our life, we must cast it from us :—when it is mere obstruction, we may often push it aside as a surface decay, breaking through it by the budding development of our life. But having for our practical need rid ourselves of it, we must then do justice to the representative value it once had, and to the old life of which it was true product, or for which it did true service. Let our Creed be the affirmation of main governing thoughts which illustrate their power and value in our human life; which, through the cravings of our life we first dimly recognise, and which, in the course of our life guided by them, become more and more clear and prized. There are times when men will be found declaring their spiritual wants and the insufficiency of creeds; echoing each other's cries, and yet not striving with proportionate energy after Creed, after spiritual certainties. That a want must be felt in society, thoroughly and long, before by the endeavour of the wise it can be fully understood and provided for, is certain; and so the outcry against Creed is neither surprising nor valueless—nevertheless, it is but a forewarning, foretelling voice. Without Creed, cannot man continue. There is Real Supreme Good. The powers that work in the world and our life, work fixedly in forms and order for good—and so spiritual certainties there are, which, unless known and felt, noble and hopeful work is impossible for man. For a creedless generation, bitter against creeds, new and energizing affirmation of spiritual truths—Creed in the high sense—is at hand.

"HOPE THAT MAKETH NOT ASHAMED."

O wondrous Lord of earth and heaven !
　The ever-living One,
From Whom perpetual life streams forth,
　As light doth from the sun ;
In Thee we ever will rejoice,
　In darken'd hours and bright—
Thou changest silence to a voice,
　And bringest day from night.

The years unbrokenly march on,
　And each is crown'd by Thee ;
Then enters as a music hall
　Thy vast eternity,
And when the years all gather'd are
　The music shall begin,
And sound shall vanquish silence there,
　As love doth vanquish sin.

And as a valley dim and dark,
　When now above each hill
The sun has risen in the sky,
　A golden light doth fill;
The past shall all illumin'd be,
　When hindering time above
Into Thy thought, which is the sky,
　Hath risen the sun, Thy love.

Lord, in a valley here we dwell,
　The aged mountains round,
As storms that echo, showers that fall,
　Thy varying footsteps sound;
And as the wind from mountains high,
　So comes Thy Truth from Thee;
Strong as Thy power, fresh as Thy joy,
　Sweet as Thy love can be.

And when we the sun-gilded brow
　Of the distant future see,
As stately palm-trees wave in air,
　Our spirits bend to Thee;
Need-rooted here on earth we are,
　As trees we move, we rise;
But we would be as stars that sweep
　Unhinder'd through the skies.

THE STUDY OF MAN.

Only by being man can we know man. The
more that an individual is integrally a man, the
more may he know of man. The world needs

men who are predominantly knowers; but these
men, if they shall indeed for the world service-
ably know, must have a natural human fulness,
a plentifulness of human instincts. How shall
they, who know not life, guide life? The
blindest guidance is that of those who, without
having a heart, would rule hearts. The more
deeply and widely human we are, the more
of inquiring zeal have we concerning man.
Often shall we endeavour to outline some provinces of human nature, and shall have result
from our study that is true aid for its own
furtherance; loving our map, though the towns
on it be dots, the rivers lines, the mountains
shadings. We shall rejoice too, when we attain
the rock pinnacle of some lofty truth, and survey
therefrom wide countries of reality; for though
around such heights mists often sweep, vexing
the eye and shrouding the prospect, yet gleams
of an instant may be enduring joys of the
memory; and if the quick regathering of the
mist speaks of hinderance and limitation, its
easy rending by the wind may tell also that the
veil is both removable and transient. Sometimes, in seeking a bright irradiating Thought
that shall light up the extensive and oft un-
cleared country of the Right, we shall get

gleams, through cloud, of a moon not yet at the full ; and sometimes we shall become conscious of an increasing twilight glow from a sun now rising above the mountains.

These are principal thoughts for the student of man :—That it is intended he should achieve his own good: he works in God, but he works. That all that is of necessity is of love : whatever is of the Supreme Will, is of and for good. That the stages of the advance of the world are according to the Supreme Will, though the subordinate wills, acting instrumentally, act freely. That the summation of the influences of necessity is ever prevailing for good over the summation of the influences of the evil will for evil. As the breath of the sick man, and the evil exhalations of impure places, cannot make the great atmosphere impure, but, taken up into its pureness, are dispersed, and turned to good account ; so is it with the sin-miasma from the evil will of a man, and from that of a generation. As learners concerning man and truth, we are hearers of evidence ; we may not judge fully till we have heard all ; but as we listen, the different points come out one by one, and our judgment at the last will be the summary of many lesser summations.

THE HUMAN COUNTENANCE.

How large a number of human faces are either ugly or at least unbeautiful! and yet, again, how many of these have something good in their quiet, ordinary expression, and are capable of passing aspects that have in them a certain divineness! Often we may see good in an evil countenance, cheerfulness upon a darkened one, like blue spots on a clouded sky; and as the blue spots tell us of a hidden expanse, and remind us that the cloud is but a covering, so such face-changes disclose to us something of heaven in man, and remind us that on the heavenly in man the earthly may rest but as a transient shadow. Character may transfigure countenance, as the man transfigures his dark environment of circumstance; and truth, thought, and nobleness may be written grandly upon, and, as it were, beam forth from, rough countenances worn and haggard. And so in a face you may read the story of the world, its tragedy and its hope—the overcoming of evil by good. Of some faces, the expression, when the head is raised, is full of energy and love; but, when the head is bowed, tells of much sorrow, and many strivings of the flesh and spirit :—a figure this of how it is with the same man in his different states. The earthly life, with its necessity and struggle—the heavenly, with its peace and aspiration—both have part in him ; and it is when looking heavenward that what is in him of heaven is best seen, whilst as he looks earthward the earthly most appears.

How encouraging is the phrase, " Good points in a man ! "   At first it seems not so; for we say, " Points only of good on a wide surface of evil."   But then we remember that truth and goodness throw out a vivifying electric agency, that electricity seeks the points, and by these enters and influences the mass.

With these thoughts and other kindred ones was the mind of our Theophilus busied as he sat at his window resting a few minutes after a walk of business to the city, which he had entered and left, he said, " by its gate Beautiful—the fields."   Having meditated himself into some tension and loftiness of spirit, before he rose and went to mathematic studies, he inwardly recited these verses of his :—

LIFE.

What if each world be as a seed,
  Unquicken'd till it die?

Then strike me, as we sin and bleed,
  Roots for eternity.
And the earth, as a mighty tree,
  Slow rises to the sky,
With ripening fruits, fair blossoming boughs,
  And spreading majesty.

The giant ship, Life, traverses
  A tempest-girdled deep,
And over big, cloud-darken'd waves
  Its stately course must keep ;
But far above the cloud and surge
  Blue-beaming heavens sleep,
And often on the waters dark
  To brighten them will peep.

August and solemn is Thy love,
  O God, even as Thy fear ;
Thy works oft slow as storm-clouds move,
  As terrible appear.
From dark sky-mountains breaks the fire,
  The hush'd lands thunders hear ;
In hail-noise and the roaring wind
  Doom-wrath seems drawing near.

Through storm and dark Thou workest long,
  Dost good in evil see,
And must be loved, in courage strong,
  With depth and sanctity.
Thou honourest man by strifes and pains,
  Sin-conqueror to be ;
And sternest disciplines prepare
  Most full felicity.

Till fixed we are not free. The acorn must be earthed ere the oak will develop. The man must believe ere the humanity will unfold. The man of faith is the man who has taken root—taken root in God. Christ is God's ground for man's rooting. Our works from our heart, our heart in God; this is spiritual freedom. Faith is the Christian excellence and the Christian blessing. By confidence God rewards fidelity. The will stedfast to the truth—this is fidelity. The heart assured by the truth—this is confidence. The confidence, so comfortable for man, increases as we act with the fidelity so acceptable to God. Our fidelity will not be without failures, nor our confidence without fears. But if we be of the "truth as it is in Jesus," the "love of the Spirit" works in us, both to permanise and strengthen our fidelity, and to increase and exhilarate our confidence. When the soul realizes Christ as the living truth, the will takes its cross and follows Him—the mind, with open ear, sits like Mary at His feet, to receive His wisdom—the heart, like John, leans reposingly upon His bosom. By faith, the finite and growing soul becomes ever more and more dependently one with God. And since the Soul is Will, and Mind, and Heart, faith is obedient, intelligent, and affectionate; and as we " follow on,"we endeavour, learn, and desire. And because the present world is evil, as we endeavour, we must often fail and struggle; as we learn, be perplexed and bewildered; and as we desire, pant and faint. But " draw nigh to God, and He will draw nigh to you." If we live by faith, God will be ever again visiting us with His salvation, becoming anew our Strength, our Truth, our Rest.

HYMN OF BLESSING.

" I will bless the Lord at all times ; His praise shall continually be in my mouth."

Thee will we bless when morning bright
    Doth new create our world and heart,
Sleep-changed, now from the dreamful night
    As from a chrysalid-vest we part;
In evening's valley closed our eyes,
    We wake as on a mountain high;
Vales now beneath, in front sunrise,
    Wide earth around, above the sky.

Thee will we bless when evening dusk
    With trembling flowers of light is hung;
Now seems the world a buried husk,
    Whence starry majesty hath sprung;
Now with a solemn, wondering heart,
    Fix'd, gazing up with deep desires,
Men stand, then soon in peace depart
    For wife, and child, and household fires.

Thee will we bless when noon is high,
   Earth's work, a ship with full-set sails,
Through waters striving heavily,
   By skill-bought power of wind prevails.
That great work-governor, the sun,
   Illumines now the countries wide;
Nor know we till hath rest begun,
   How many suns there are beside.

Be Thou, Lord, by the cities blest,
   Life-seas with sleeping waves of power,
Upon whose bosom so wide may rest
   Noon and dark night at one same hour.
As spirit-nebulæ, cloudy, dim,
   Full-peopled cities distant are ;
Near-by each spirit hath its beam,
   And, separate, brightens to a star.

Thee will we bless from off the sea,
   Thine ancient water-empire wide :
Far-thundering waves unrestingly
   Lift to the light, in darkness hide.
They hear the mighty wind-king's voice,
   Thy captain winds their force control,
In swelling vastness they rejoice
   When Thou commandest them to roll.

Thee will we bless upon the land,
   The embellish'd earth, complete and fair ;
To all the creatures of Thine hand
   Thy love is an encircling air.

The forest dark, the mountain strong,
   Thou didst prepare in deeps of time;
Of energy and beauty young,
   Thy works appear in every clime.

Thou, Lord, art by the seasons blest—
   The hoary-headed Winter old—
Spring, with her green flower-border'd vest—
   Autumn in many-shaded gold—
The Summer clothed in richest blue,
   Her seamless robe the heaven pure;
These changing rule, all countries through,
   Their beauty and Thy praise endure.

Thee bless we for the sun-bright name—
   Christ, which on earth's great heart we trace,
Love-written, a word of burning flame,
   Which He may darken or efface,
Who with His breath shall quench the sun
   As easily as a quivering spark:
And circling worlds plunge every one
   Deep back into the wintry dark.

O God! when from the darken'd sky
   Wind-broken clouds the sun doth melt,
Sweet rains and rainbows' majesty,
   Thy powers of Life and Hope are felt;
Then bless we Good which evil sways,
   In fathomless wisdom all Divine:
Above our weather-changing days
   Still doth Thy Mercy's heaven shine.

We have often visited Trinal when he resided
at Barrenhill—a place, as he said, " where brood-
ing darkness spreads her jealous wings ; " an
unspiritual place, dull and old, but with radiant
country about it—" like a glory," Theophilus
said, " round the head of a simpleton." Here
he lived at Blackberry Bush Cottage—so he
named it; for he would have it, that a blackberry
bush is one of the best emblems for man ; " its
fruits," said he, " so rarely ripen all and ripen
well, and on it sweet berries are so frequently
found side by side with harsh ones." We
remember his taking up some of the manuscript
from which we have since compiled these Memorials. As he turned the pages, sometimes he
sighed, and sometimes a bright flush passed over
his countenance. "Many things are but hinted
in these papers," said he. " They would make
but a fragmentary book." " Nevertheless, there
might be a blessing in it," said we, as if vindi-
cating our own after-work of editor ; " a blessing
as of a shower which falls dispersedly, driven by
winds, and irregularly lessening and increasing
its force ; it means kindly to the earth, and the
earth receives it not without thankfulness. The
days of May and June are debtors to the many-
weathered day of April." We knew that there

was much Trinal was striving to perfect, and hoping one day to speak on Christian theology, which was not to be found in these papers; and we told him so. "Yes, indeed," he replied. Then, after a few moments' silence, he repeated, with unusual emphasis, his favourite words: "Oh, rest in the Lord! Wait patiently for Him, and He shall give to thee thine heart's desires." And then he said, "Will you walk awhile with me?"

THE END.

www.ingramcontent.com/pod-product-compliance
Lightning Source LLC
Chambersburg PA
CBHW021805110726
47902CB00006B/1658